A.B. Freeman-Mitford

The Bamboo Garden

A.B. Freeman-Mitford

The Bamboo Garden

ISBN/EAN: 9783337091200

Printed in Europe, USA, Canada, Australia, Japan

Cover: Foto ©Andreas Hilbeck / pixelio.de

More available books at **www.hansebooks.com**

THE

BAMBOO GARDEN

BY

A. B. FREEMAN-MITFORD, C.B.

AUTHOR OF 'TALES OF OLD JAPAN'

ILLUSTRATED BY ALFRED PARSONS

London

MACMILLAN AND CO., Ltd.

NEW YORK: MACMILLAN & CO.

1896

TO

SIR JOSEPH HOOKER, K.C.S.I., C.B., F.R.S.

THIS LITTLE BOOK IS DEDICATED WITH

AFFECTION AND RESPECT

PREFACE

THIS little book has no scientific pretensions. It is simply an attempt to give a descriptive list, what the French call a *catalogue raisonné*, of the hardy Bamboos in cultivation in this country, and to focus such information in regard to them as could be obtained from Japanese as well as from European sources, and was therefore not readily available to the general public. Some of the matter has already appeared in a series of articles which I published last year in the *Garden* newspaper; but all of these have been revised and corrected, while the descriptions of species have been almost entirely rewritten. The task has not been an easy one, and would have been impossible but for the very kind encouragement and assistance which I have received from Sir Joseph Hooker and Mr. Thiselton Dyer, the director of Kew Gardens. I have also to acknowledge the help so cordially given by Messrs. Nicholson, Watson, and Bean of Kew Gardens. The latter gentleman's articles on Hardy Bamboos which appeared in the *Gardeners' Chronicle* in 1894 contain much valuable information. Some of the chief growers of Bamboos in this country, notably Lord Annesley, Lord de Saumarez, Sir Edmund Loder, the Right Hon. A. Smith-Barry, M.P., and Mr. Rashleigh of Menabilly have very kindly communicated to me their experiences of Bamboo cultivation in various parts of these islands. M. Latour-Marliac, of Temple-sur-Lot, Lot-et-Garonne, France, the greatest European importer of these plants, has always been most amiably ready to furnish me with the results of his observations. To all of these gentlemen my thanks are due.

Messrs. Rivière's beautifully illustrated book, *Les Bambous*, and the late General Munro's monograph, published in *The Transactions of the Linnean Society*, 15th November 1866, are respectively the French and English classics upon the subject. I have not hesitated to draw largely upon such rich storehouses of knowledge; but since the publication of those works many new species have been discovered, and they are therefore not up to date, otherwise there would be no reason for any further book treating of Bamboos.

One attraction, at any rate, I may claim for my book in the admirable drawings so kindly furnished by Mr. Alfred Parsons, whose life-long devotion to the portraiture of plant life found a new scope in the flora and landscape of Japan, of which his transcripts by pen and pencil have charmed the reading and the artist world of England and America.

24th February 1896.

CONTENTS

CHAPTER VII

CHAPTER VIII

LIST QF ILLUSTRATIONS

ERRATA

P. 14, line 10, *for* " more productive " *read* " non-reproductive."

,, line 28, *after* " first year" *for* comma *substitute* colon.

P. 40, line 20, *for* " Colloquois" *read* " Colloquios."

P. 90, line 12, *for* " three sides, there " *read* " three sides : these."

P. 93, line 13, *after* " brilliant " *insert* " green."

P. 96, line 6, *for* " later" *read* " latter."

P. 172, line 19, *after* " leaves " *insert* " which are tessellated.'

CHAPTER I

THE BAMBOO GARDEN

Arundinaria Japonica.

I F there be one feature which more than any other distinguishes our modern gardens from the trim pleasaunces in which our forebears took their ease, playing their rubber of bowls decorously on lawns hemmed in by Yew hedges as stiff as their own ruffs, it is the value given to beauty of form in plants as apart from that of colour. No one who has seen at their best the giants and pigmies of the Bamboo family will deny their supreme loveliness in this respect. The stately spears of Phyllostachys mitis, the Brobdingnagian plumes

B

of Arundinaria Simoni, the trembling grace of Phyllostachys Henonis or P. viridi-glaucescens, not to speak of
many others, have added to our borders, our shrubberies,
and more especially to our wild gardens, a wealth of
beauty which a few years ago would have been deemed
beyond the craziest dreams of the enthusiast. It needed
the energy and enterprise of such collectors as Messrs.
Veitch, the brothers Villa of Genoa, and above all
M. Latour-Marliac of Temple-sur-Lot (a name which will
always be associated with the hybridisation of Water-Lilies)
to establish the fact that, even if we may not hope to
see our Bamboos grow to the huge dimensions which they
attain in their native countries, there are many the hardiness
of which is proof against our severest winters. Surrounded
as the present writer is by a great number of varieties of
these famous Grasses, it is impossible for him to doubt
their powers of resistance. They have stood through four
winters and 26° of frost; they have resisted an even more
deadly enemy than frost in the droughts of 1892, 1893, and
1895. In the more congenial summer of 1894 they shot
into life with a vigour which gave the best promise for a
future when they shall have been thoroughly established.
But, alas! the great Sun-God, who should have ripened the
shoots, hid his face throughout the year, and when the grim
winter of 1895 set in the culms had not the enduring power
to resist its attacks. All the tallest shoots of Phyllostachys
mitis perished, and many species were badly cut. Evidently,
moreover, what took place above ground was only a repetition
of the havoc which was going on underground. The rhizomes,
which must have made rare growth during a wet summer and

an autumn which lasted beyond Christmas (witness the roses!), can have been no more ripened than the culms, and must have been cruelly pinched when at last the frost came armed with its iron nippers. As a matter of consequence, the first shoots of 1895 were not as strong as they would have been but for this combination of adversities. The normal yearly increase in the size of the young plants was not observable. But there was no falling out of the ranks, not a single species, hardly a single plant was lost; and now at the end of a hot but terribly dry summer the plants have increased in bulk, if not in height, and hope again tells the most flattering of tales.

From all quarters—I am writing only of places under the normal climate of England, and not of the favoured regions of the Far West and South—the same report reaches me: a severe check, but no deaths. As for Phyllostachys nigra, nigropunctata, Boryana, Henonis, and viridi-glaucescens, they simply laughed at the thermometer, and were as bright at the end of the winter as at midsummer.

Hitherto our plants have had to struggle for bare existence against every disadvantage. Ruthlessly torn from their native soil, sent away with hardly so much root as would furnish an adequate knob to a walking-stick, condemned to undergo the horrors of a journey of several weeks by sea and by land without light, air, moisture, or soil, what wonder if the poor home-sick starvelings have found it a hard matter to retain a spark of life in a strange land, where they find neither the glorious sunshine nor the bounteous rains which gave them birth? But the fight is over now and the victory is won. The death-roll is practically nil, and the survivors are thriving peacefully, accommodating themselves to new and altogether strange conditions of existence, proof, to all appearance, against any treachery which the climate of the Cotswold Hills may bring to bear upon them. We need not despair of seeing in a few years miniature groves of Bamboos clothed in all their marvellous grace, and lacking no native beauty, save only at night the myriad darting lamps of the fire-flies, by whose light, as the pretty fable runs, Confucius and his disciples used to study.

Up to the present the nomenclature of the Bamboos is more or less in a fog, and of the many varieties grown here some will doubtless prove to be identical with others sent out under a different name. Making allowance, however, for this, there will yet be nearly fifty distinct types which may be successfully cultivated in all but the most inclement and exposed portions of our islands. From the horticultural, in contradistinction to the botanical, point of view it may be hoped that the determination of the relationship of the various species to one another may never be arrived at here ; for this can only be attained with accuracy by the inflorescence, and when the Bamboo flowers and fruits it dies, or at best is so weakened that it takes years to recover its pristine vigour.

Messrs. Auguste and Charles Rivière, in their treatise on Bamboos, observe that a large number of the family, unlike the rest of the Gramineæ, are very miserly in the production of their flowers, which they only show at long intervals— sometimes of more than thirty years, and they cite Colonel Munro and others in support of this assertion. Humboldt says that Mutis, during twenty years of botanical work in the swampy forests of the Bambusa guadua, never once saw it in flower. Roxburgh only once came across the flowers of Bambusa Balcoa. On the other hand, the male Bamboo (Dendrocalamus strictus), Dendrocalamus edulis, Arundinaria Hookeriana and some others, flower every year. But the most noteworthy phenomenon is the simultaneous flowering of certain Bamboos. When the given moment has come round, every plant of the same species, whether old or young, over a vast region will put forth its flowers at one and the same moment, and, having seeded, for a time the plant disappears. Auguste St. Hilaire, the botanist who explored Brazil, mentions a forest of the Toboca, a gramineous plant, where he was entranced by the aërial beauty of the long canes, from 40 to 50 feet high, bending in elegant arches, crossing one another in every direction, tangling their huge panicles and giving glimpses of the deep blue sky through a spreading and diaphanous web of foliage. "The plant was then in flower. When I passed that way a few months later the forest had disappeared." Colonel Munro called attention to the reports upon this subject contained in vols. xiii. and xiv. of the *Journal of the Agricultural and Horticultural Society of India.* Sir W. Sleeman records the fact observed by him that in 1836 all the great Bamboos, which for twenty-five years had been the most beautiful feature of the valley Dehra Dun, between the Ganges and the Jumna to the south-west of Gurwhal, began to flower and seed—canes which had only been transplanted during the previous season following the example of their twenty-year-old mates— after which all perished together. Wallich tells of a grove of Bamboos surrounding the town of Rampore, in Rohilcund, which flowered and died in 1824. He was informed that the same thing had happened forty years previously. In 1839, according to Spilsbury, all the Bamboos between Jubbulpore and Mundlah died soon after flowering. Similar annihilations of whole forests of Bamboos are noted in the case of Melocanna bambusoides, which disappeared after flowering throughout Tipperah, at Runipore, Arraca, and Chittagong, causing a great inconvenience and loss in Tipperah through the want of Bamboos for building. All the famous botanists —Humboldt, Bonpland, Roxburgh, Mutis, Spence, Wallich, Spilsbury, Gray, Hooker, Brandis, Bory de St. Vincent, Auguste St. Hilaire, and others who have travelled through the Bamboo forests—are agreed in confirming the facts given above as to the simultaneous flowering of the species, the death of the plants after flowering or seeding, and the rare recurrence of the flowering period in most species, a fact which sufficiently explains the uncertainty which surrounds the nomenclature of the Bamboos which are now cultivated in Europe.

On the other hand, as against these observations, Dr. Anderson, superintendent of the Botanic Gardens at Calcutta, reports that in 1857 and 1858 many Bamboos flowered and seeded near Calcutta, when, contrary to expectation, there was no general mortality among the plants. So far as he was able to ascertain, only the culms which had flowered perished, and were replaced by young shoots which came from the roots; but before flowering and seeding, the foliage of the canes almost entirely disappeared. He further states that in 1861, when Bambusa gigantea flowered for the first time for thirty years, the plants, though weakened, lived.

Having dealt with the suicidal mystery of the flower of

the Bamboos in their own country, Messrs. Rivière proceed to examine the phenomenon as it has been observed in Europe. It appears that in 1867 or 1868 flowers began to appear on two fine clumps of Arundinaria japonica (Bambusa Métaké) in the Bois de Boulogne ; at the same moment they were noticed on the same species in the nursery gardens of Messrs. Thibaut and Keteleer at Sceaux, at Marseilles, in the pleasure grounds of M. Paulin Talabot, and in other European collections. What is more strange is that the infection crossed the Mediterranean, for the plants of Arundinaria japonica in the Government gardens of the Hamma at Algiers flowered in concert with their European brethren; and not only did the whole of the canes, old as well as young, bear flowers together, but the very shoots as they showed above the soil were transformed into flowering stems. Yet were the plants not altogether killed, though weakened and exhausted by this exaggerated inflorescence. The new shoots were but from 3 to 4 inches high, and even these were covered with flowers. For a long time the plants remained paralysed. Still, careful nursing and coddling saved the few rhizomes which had resisted the epidemic ; the species was preserved, and in 1878 the canes had reached a height of from 10 to 12 feet. In 1875 M. Carrière noted in the *Revue Horticole* the appearance in the autumn of that year of flowers on Arundinaria falcata [1] in Brittany and Normandy. The plants at Angers, at Nantes, and in Algiers followed suit. In March and April 1876, those in the garden of the Luxem-

[1] Under the description of THAMNOCALAMUS FALCONERI will be found my reasons for supposing that these plants which flowered over France and in Algiers were THAMNOCALAMUS FALCONERI, and not ARUNDINARIA FALCATA.

bourg, even the specimens in pots, did the same. Mr.
Osborne, gardener to Mr. Smith-Barry at Fota Island, Co.
Cork, writes me word that his plants of Thamnocalamus
Falconeri, then named Arundinaria falcata, flowered and
fruited the same year. His diary for 11th August 1876
records the gathering of Bamboo seeds. A third instance
has been recorded in the case of Phyllostachys flexuosa.
It was in the garden of the Hamma at Algiers that the
flowers first made their appearance in the month of February
1876. In the month of May following they were observed
at Toulon in M. Turrel's garden, and in July in Messrs.
Thibaut and Keteleer's nursery at Sceaux and in the Jardin
d'Acclimatation in Paris. Allowance being made for the
difference of climate, it is evident that these plants practically
flowered together. In these three species it was remarked
that immediately before flowering the leaves turned yellow,
withered, and fell off, to be replaced by the inflorescence.

Now comes the question whether it is to be taken as
proven that the Bamboo after flowering and fruiting
necessarily dies. Some eminent botanists, as we have seen,
have described the death of whole forests of Bamboos from
this cause; others hold a contrary opinion, notably Dr.
Anderson, who observed the exhaustion of the plant after
flowering, but saw the new growth spring from the roots.
In the cases recorded above of the flowering of Arundinaria
falcata (or Thamnocalamus Falconeri) and Arundinaria
japonica, the canes died, but new buds came from the
roots. In the case of Phyllostachys flexuosa, new stems
came in the same way. It is true that the plants suffered
greatly from exhaustion, but they did not perish.

On the whole, modern opinion appears to incline to the belief that the older botanists and travellers came to rather hasty conclusions in this matter, which could only be determined by protracted observations on the spot. For instance, take St. Hilaire's case of the vanished forest of Toboca. What happened in the ensuing season? Were the plants renewed? There is nothing to show. How are the forests renewed? Hardly by seed, for the seed falling on a soil encumbered with the remains and roots of the dead plants would scarcely find the nourishment essential to its successful germination. Moreover, experience shows that even in the wildest nature one kind of tree, if destroyed, is followed by another totally different species. Is it not more probable that, given the wonderful powers of vegetation under the conditions of tropical rain and sun, the rhizomes having preserved some degree of vitality should quickly replace the dead by living canes? Sir Joseph Hooker, in a passage of his *Himalayan Journals* quoted below in Chapter IV., distinctly states that the small Bamboo Praong sends up many flowering branches from the root, and "after maturing its seed and *giving off suckers from the root*, the parent plant dies." That is the point—"*after giving off suckers from the root.*" Surely this is strong evidence in favour of the theory that the Bamboos generally do not reproduce themselves solely by seed. If we consider what a stemless particle of Squitch root will do in our climate, it needs no great effort of the imagination to realise the rampant power of growth in the rhizomes of these monstrous Couch Grasses in the Tropics, or in those countries, like China and Japan, where the rainy season occurs during the great heats of summer. This, at any rate, is the view to which their unrivalled experience in the gardens of the Hamma at Algiers has led Messrs. Rivière.

We should note that, although in late years large importations of all manner of Bamboos have taken place, at the time when the simultaneous flowering of Arundinaria japonica (Bambusa Métaké) took place, the whole of the plants then in cultivation in Europe and at Algiers were but offsets of the parent plant introduced by Siebold in 1850. It may be urged, therefore, that it was in truth one and the same plant, reaching maturity at the same moment in its various parts, wherever those parts might be distributed. Possibly the same may be said of Arundinaria falcata (or Thamnocalamus Falconeri) and Phyllostachys flexuosa. Even so, the wonder is great.

It might at first be imagined that the period of flowering would recur at regular fixed intervals, when the Bamboo has reached the length of its tether to life; but Sir Joseph Hooker in his *Himalayan Journals*, p. 107 (ed. 1891), says, "At about 4000 feet" (on Mount Tonglo, near Darjeeling) "the great Bamboo (Pao Lepcha) abounds; it flowers every year, which is not the case with all others of this genus, most of which flower profusely over large tracts of country once in a great many years, and then die away, their place being supplied by seedlings which grow with immense rapidity. This well-known fact is not due, as some suppose, to the life of the species being of such a duration, but to favourable circumstances in the season." It used to be commonly said by natives of Bamboo-growing countries that the plants flowered once in thirty years, and that the age of a man might be determined from the number of times that he had witnessed the phenomenon. It is, however, now established that the flowering is variable, infrequent, and due to climatic causes.

Arundinaria Simoni furnishes one exception of a Bamboo which flowers in England without dying. It has not infrequently borne seed in this country, and has been apparently none the worse. Last year (1895) it flowered and seeded in more than one English garden. I myself gathered seed from one culm of a large clump in a garden in Surrey. The remaining culms were all in their normal condition, and there was no sign of the leafy stems being replaced by flower-bearing branchlets, or of any injury to, or exhaustion of, the plant.

CHAPTER II

THE following observations are taken almost entirely from
Messrs. Rivière's very able treatise. Personally I have had
but a very limited experience in Bamboo propagation. Nor
indeed, for obvious reasons, climatic and other, is it very
likely that it will ever be a successful industry in most parts
of this country, though if seed could be obtained it would
not be a difficult matter. In Cornwall, however, and other
favoured localities where the climate is not very different
from that of Japan, and where it follows that root action
must be far more free than it is in the Midlands, I have little
doubt that the methods recommended by Messrs. Rivière
might be followed with most profitable results by nursery
gardeners. There is a large and growing demand for the
plants; they are expensive and difficult to obtain—in many
instances we are compelled to seek them in foreign nurseries—
and I feel sure that any enterprising man, taking advantage
of the rare opportunities afforded by the conditions of soil
and climate in the far west of our island, and in parts of
Ireland, would reap a rich harvest by starting this new
industry. To send to Japan, or even to the South of France,
for plants is an expensive and risky process. Why should

our own gardeners not have the profit which now goes abroad?

The hardy Bamboos may be propagated in any one of four ways :—

1. By seed.
2. By division.
3. By cuttings of the base of the culm, with or without the rhizome attached.
4. By cuttings of rhizomes.

A fifth process, propagation by layering, is available in the case of the autumn-growing or tender Bamboos, but it is impossible in the case of the whole family of Triglossæ to which our hardy Bamboos belong. It may be well before going any further, in order to save beginners from the disappointment of a vain attempt, to explain the reason of this impossibility. The two or three knots at the base of the stem, which are close together and barren of branches, contain in a potential state the bud from which a new culm springs upward and the roots shoot downwards. The upper knots contain no such buds; they carry only their two or more branches which are absolutely barren and unproductive. As it is, of course, the upper part of the stem which would be bent down to the ground for layering, it follows that the effort must be abortive. Endless experiments conducted by Messrs. Rivière in Algiers have resulted only in proving the futility of the attempt. It is not uncommon to see a new culm shoot out of a branchless knot of the base of a mature stem. Great care must be taken not to brush against or interfere with this young growth. The roots do not develop downward until after it has ripened, and the attachment is exceedingly brittle. I have before me such a culm which was snapped off by a hen pheasant; it is fully branched, but much smaller than the parent stem. At its base are two new knots ready apparently to start into life; the verticillate roots are on the point of taking their downward course. Had that end been accomplished, the new stem would have been safely fixed in the ground. In its frail condition it fell a victim to the rush of a frightened bird.

This more productive character of the upper branches goes to show that the method of planting horizontally adopted by some Bamboo growers cannot be so advantageous as they believe it to be. I have seen it asserted that by laying newly-received Bamboos horizontally in the ground roots are struck and culms formed all along the stem. I have never tried the method myself, though I intend to do so as an experiment. But it seems to me that, in the case of the Triglossæ, Messrs. Rivière have established the fact that, at most, roots and new culms could only be produced from the few branchless nodes at the base of the stem.

1. PROPAGATION BY SEED.—Owing to the rarity of the occurrence of the fruit—which, indeed, in some species has not yet come under the observation of science—this must always be the least used method. On one occasion indeed we received some seed of a Bamboo under the name of Bambusa siamensis, probably from its habitat a tender species, which germinated freely, but which we did not succeed in rearing beyond the first year, with the same seed Kew fared no better. We also raised from seed a number of plants of the Burmese Bamboo (Dendrocalamus membrana-

ceus)—scarcely a grain missed fire—but we have never yet
been able to get ripe seed of any of the hardy species.
The seed should be sown sparsely in pans filled with garden
soil—the more silicate it contains the better—and well
drained with broken potsherds or stones. Cover the seed
with fine soil about a quarter of an inch deep or less. If the
seed be sown too thickly, the development of the young plant
is hindered. Water well with a very fine rose until the
whole soil be thoroughly soaked. The pans should be placed
in hotbeds and frequently watered, great care being taken to
prevent the soil from drying. The frames should be partially
shaded from the sun and kept fairly ventilated, more air
being admitted as the seedlings gain strength. Assuming the
seed to have been sown in the latter end of March or in
April, the young plants may bear full exposure to air and
sun in June. In the following spring the plants should be
pricked out into 3-inch pots, which, after generous watering,
again should be placed under glass upon a hotbed to help
the plants to root in their new abode. At first the outer air
should be excluded or very sparingly admitted. By degrees
they will bear longer exposure, until in the latter end of May
or early June the pots are plunged in open beds, buried a
little below the surface, and covered with a mulching of dead
leaves or straw. The beds should be well watered during
the summer. In the month of October the pots must be
taken up and placed in a cool or temperate house, or under
cold frames, which must be covered up during severe frosts.
In the month of May following they may be planted out in
their permanent places. The very slight variations necessary
if the seed should not be sown until the summer or autumn

will be patent to every gardener. In the latter case germination may possibly not take place until the following spring, and even then it may be advisable to help it by again having recourse to the hotbed. In all cases be it remembered that moisture is the first essential element of success.

2. PROPAGATION BY DIVISION.—The best moment for this operation is, in our climate, the latter end of April. The process is very simple. The plants should be divided into clumps of two or three culms with their rhizome, in order to ensure a new growth from the buds on the internodes of the root-stock. If the tufts can be lifted with a ball of earth, so much the better. They should be planted in beds at distances of 2 feet, carefully watered, and protected by a top-dressing of well-rotted cow manure and dead leaves. With the same care they may be planted at once in their permanent homes.

3. PROPAGATION BY CUTTINGS OF THE BASE OF THE CULM WITH OR WITHOUT THE RHIZOME ATTACHED.—Cut off about a foot's length of rhizome bearing a stem; cut down the stem to about the same length. Plant at such a depth as will ensure the two or three lowest and branchless knots at the base of the culm being covered with earth. This may be effected either in pots or in the open ground. It is essential that the stem should be cut down, otherwise it begins to wither downwards; a sort of creeping paralysis of the whole plant ensues, ending in death. Reproduction is also possible without the attached rhizome, and this method is specially valuable where, owing to the rarity of the plant or for other reasons, economy is an object. For the rhizome

being left in its place continues its work of multiplication undisturbed. We have seen above that the lower knots, occurring at short intervals and barren of all ramification, are each furnished with verticillated roots and a reproductive bud ; indeed, the former may often be seen falling downwards to the earth in a little cascade all round the culm, sometimes burying themselves and rooting in the ground, at others remaining in an abortive or embryonic condition. This reproductive power may be turned to account by cutting the stem with a very sharp instrument as close to the rhizome as possible. The stem is then cut back and the lower nodes buried in a pot, allowing only the end of the last branchless internode to protrude. Slight warmth and moisture are all that is required to ensure rooting. The operation should be performed in the spring, and by the end of the year a new plant will have been obtained.

4. PROPAGATION BY CUTTINGS OF RHIZOMES.—This is a very simple process. It takes place in the spring, and consists merely of lifting the rhizomes, cutting them into lengths of from 6 inches to 8 inches, which are planted at a depth of from 4 inches to 6 inches in good rich loam and copiously watered during the summer. Care should be taken to see that each length, which will have three or four knots, should be the growth only of the preceding year, containing living eyes or buds, for the older rhizomes are sterile, those buds which have not shot up into canes having withered still-born. It is therefore only the young rhizome which is reproductive.

If the end to be attained be commercial the third and

the fourth of these methods are those which will recommend
themselves to those who desire to propagate Bamboos in
this country; and in that case potting will be substituted
for open ground cultivation; in other respects the procedure
will be the same.

CHAPTER III

BAMBOOS are hungry plants and well repay generous treatment. They should be planted in rich loam, not too stiff, and for the first year or two should be well mulched. A good plan is to cover the roots with a liberal dressing of cow manure, adding a thick layer of dead leaves on the top. This protects them from frost in winter, and, by preventing evaporation, keeps the underground stems moist in summer. In order to prevent the leaves from being blown away and to keep out rabbits, the clump should be surrounded with wire netting. In three or four years, when the plants shall have been thoroughly established and made good growth, they may be left to take care of themselves, but they need a little coddling at first. Where water is available they should be well irrigated during the period of growth, but a wet place is very hurtful and often fatal to them in winter when the frost sets in. The more they are sheltered from wind the better; especially must they be protected from our cutting north-easterly winds in spring. Plants that have to face the terrors of the typhoon in their own country are not so liable to be injured by the softer and damper southerly and south-westerly winds. Still, shelter

is a great object. It often happens, especially in the case
of the more flexible Bamboos (such as Phyllostachys Henonis,
or viridi-glaucescens, for instance), that the culms, which in
a young state are extremely slender and delicate, just at
the moment when they have grown to a level with the
older stems are flogged by the latter under a gale of wind
so that their tops are destroyed, and in this way the year's
gain in height is lost. The plants, it is true, do not suffer
in health, but it is a great disappointment not to see the
new culms like spears overtopping the arched plumes
of the previous year. This mischief was very observable
here during the late summer of 1895. After the exceptionally hard winter and the drought of early summer,
the new culms of Phyllostachys Henonis did not start
into growth until late in July. In one clump, too much
exposed to the south-westerly gales which raged with
great violence some five or six weeks later, all the tender
points were beaten back and the plants are no higher than
they were last year. This is a danger to guard against.
Therefore again I say, shelter is a great object.

A rich, warm spot with partial shade and a good screen
on the north and east, especially under the influence of sea
air, is the true home of the Bamboo. Sea mists bring
moisture to the leaves and are Nature's syringe. Nothing
revives the plants more thoroughly, or more effectually
brings out the brilliancy which is one of their characteristics.
The worst living enemies of the plants, especially of the
dwarf species, appear to be the rats and voles, which
will burrow under the wire netting and gnaw through
the stems in order to carry away the leaves for linings

to their nests.   It is not easy to suggest any remedy for this nuisance.

From the landscape gardener's point of view it seems almost unnecessary to say that a good background is of the first importance to show off the beauty of the Bamboo. A bay in a clump of Hollies or Evergreens will afford the most appropriate setting.   The tall culms waving their dainty green foliage against such a backing, under the influence of a gentle summer breeze, are the embodiment of all that is graceful, while the tender leaves look like a flight of the most delicate green butterflies hovering in the air.   A group planted on a lawn may be very effective, but Bamboos are seen at their best when their gracefully bending culms are shown in contrast against stiffer and darker foliage.   If such a position can be found on the banks of running water, with here and there a rugged moss-grown rock cropping out of the hillside, there you have the ideal composition dear to the Japanese landscape painter.   Great care must be taken to assign to those sorts which are rampant at the roots (such as Arundinaria Métaké, Arundinaria Simoni, and some others) isolated positions where they may run riot as they please. Failing this precaution, there will in a very short time be endless work and trouble in checking their invasions. Above all let the groups be as big as may be suitable, but do not mix the species.   Let each variety stand out by itself.   As Mr. Bean says, " If this is not attended to, and the spreading rhizomes kept within certain bounds, the different kinds run into each other, and the whole eventually becomes a hopeless jungle."

Messrs. Rivière and M. Marliac both recommend that

Bamboos on being planted should be cut down. The latter even advises that the branches should be shortened back. The *Encyclopædia Britannica*, without, however, giving any authority, says: "Various expedients are followed (by the Chinese) to obtain good Bamboos, one of the most usual being to take a vigorous root and transplant it, leaving only 4 inches or 5 inches above the joint next the ground. The cavity is then filled with a mixture of horse litter and sulphur. According to the vigour of the root the shoots will be more or less numerous; they are destroyed at an early stage during three successive years, and those springing in the fourth resemble the parent tree." It may seem presumptuous to question such high authorities. Still, difference of soil and climate must count for something, and it must be borne in mind that plants in an enfeebled condition after a long journey may require different treatment from that which is suitable for those which are being propagated in their full vigour upon the spot. Certain it is that I have never cut down an imported Bamboo stem without having reason to regret it. In 1893, the Royal Gardens at Kew and myself imported a number of the same plants (Bambusa Mazeli or Quilioi) from Genoa. They were fine stems, about 10 feet high. My plants were cut down, the Kew plants were not. Although mine had if anything the advantage over the others as regards soil, they all died save two, which are feebly struggling for life, while their fellow-travellers at Kew are arching high overhead in all the pride of strength and beauty. Lord de Saumarez, who, like myself, has had experience in the cultivation of Bamboos both at home and in Japan, writes to me as follows: "In transplanting I have never followed the recommendations of Rivière to cut the plants down, but have never yet lost a clump from omitting the precaution." On the other hand, I have lost several clumps by adopting it, and on the whole I have come to the conclusion that what may be very suitable in China, in Algiers, or even in the South of France, is not advisable in this country, nor where it is a question of coaxing sickly plants into vigour.

Above all things I would warn my readers against planting out imported Bamboos in their permanent places before they have recovered from the effects of the journey. I have myself lost many fine specimens in this way. Now that a sad experience has taught me how to treat them, I rarely lose one. The plants should only travel during the period when they are at rest. They will be received, therefore, during the late autumn or winter. If they have come from abroad, the balls of earth round the roots should be thoroughly soaked ; they should then be potted and placed in a cool house for the winter ; the leaves, or bare culms if the leaves be lost, should be copiously syringed twice a day, but the roots should not be kept too wet. In this way many species will keep their leaves as green and fresh as if they had never been disturbed. One consignment which I received from Japan had made growth on the voyage, and the leaves were blanched as white as paper ; but in a few days, under the action of light, they became as brilliant in colour as their out-door neighbours. Those that lose their leaves, will early in February show signs of flourishing. The tiny buds in the axils of the branchlets will swell and fatten, leafy fronds will soon be developed, and in a month or six weeks

the plants will be in full spring beauty. Early in May
begin to harden off the plants as you would geraniums for
bedding out, and at the end of the month, or in the first days
of June, place them in their permanent homes.

When you take the plants out of the pots be careful not
to disturb the roots in any way. You must not attempt to
comb them out as you would the roots of trees, for they are
as brittle as glass; place them in the earth as they are, be
they never so pot-bound, and they will soon find their way
about. If possible, the newly-planted Bamboos should be
well watered during growth. It must be remembered that
Bamboos will not show their true characteristics for two or
three years, or even more in the case of Phyllostachys mitis;
but by taking the above precautions many disappointments
will be avoided. I have no hesitation in saying that certain
plants which I treated in this manner on their arrival last
November, and planted out last June, are now, in their
first year, quite equal to others of the same species which
have been wrestling with misfortune for four years.

Take heed to prepare a good and comfortable bed for
your Bamboos. The earth should be double dug, and if it be
done before the winter sets in, so much the better; for the
frost will break up the clods and make the soil light and
friable so that the rhizomes may travel, as it is their nature
to do, without let or hindrance. This is a great matter.
Another caution to be given is as to the manner of planting.
In treading in the plants, care must be taken not to let the
foot strike against the earth which has come out of the pots
with the Bamboos. Tread round it, but not on it. Indeed,
the less treading there is the better, for you never know

how near the top the new shoots may be ; and the usual plan
of dancing an Indian war-dance on the roots in a pair of
hob-nailed boots may destroy a year's growth. It is best to
consolidate the plants by watering freely, which thus serves
a double purpose. Bamboos planted according to these
simple and very obvious rules, and protected, as I have
suggested above, by a good warm jacket of dried leaves lined
with cow manure, will during the summer make strong
roots and good growth, and will lay in a stock of health
before having to face the miseries of an English winter.

As regards the transplanting of established clumps from
one part of the same garden to another, *not for sending them
on a journey*, this is an operation which is best undertaken
in May or June, when the new shoots first show signs of life.
Mr. Bean, writing to the *Gardeners' Chronicle* of 10th February
1894, says : "From October to March is the worst time ;
July is even better than February. Last summer I shifted
three large clumps of Arundinaria Simoni in July, which
never showed the least check." Here, at Batsford, we have
moved large plants of Phyllostachys aurea in July, August,
and September. Great care was taken to secure good balls.
The holes into which the plants were transferred were well
watered, and the roots were mulched with cow manure and
leaves. The growth of the canes was not arrested, and new
shoots, the existence of which was not suspected, continued
to appear. Our greatest disaster was sustained in March
1892, when we had the audacity to plant out a consignment
of mitis, Quilioi, viridi-glaucescens, nigra, and Narihira, all
good hardy sorts, but very few survived the fierce attacks of
the next six weeks. Another mistake made was in im-

mediately placing in their permanent positions some hundreds
of Bamboos of different sorts received from the South of France
in the month of November 1891. The chief sufferers were
mitis, nigra, and viridi-glaucescens. Had these been potted [1]
for the winter and kept indoors, as I have recommended
above, many valuable lives would have been spared, and in
all cases a great saving of time would have been effected.
It is not pleasant to acknowledge failures, but a chronicle of
errors is sometimes more instructive than the most jubilant
record of success.

[1] In transplanting into their permanent positions Bamboos which have
been grown in pots, if the roots protrude from the pot, break the pot rather
than disturb them.

CHAPTER IV

THERE is not in the whole vegetable kingdom a plant which is so intimately bound up with the life of mankind as the Bamboo. In India, Ceylon, China, Japan, the Malay Archipelago, and in the tropical forests the world over it is a servant-of-all-work.

More than one case is recorded where the abundant seeds of the Bamboo have been the means of staving off the horrors of an Indian famine. In Orissa, in 1812, when one of those rare general flowerings of the Bamboo, to which allusion has been made, took place, there was famine in the land. The seeds of the Bamboo, cooked and eaten like rice, gave their only food to many thousands. Day and night the people watched to gather the precious fruit as it fell. Mr. Shaw Stewart, the collector of Canara, on the western coast of India, states that "In 1864 there was a general flowering of the Bamboo in the Soopa jungles, and a very large number of persons, estimated at 50,000, came from the Dharwar and Belgaum districts to collect the seed. Each party remained about ten or fourteen days, taking away enough for their own consumption during the monsoon months, as well as some for sale," and adds, that "the flowering was a most

providential benefit during the prevalent scarcity." Mr.
Gray, writing from Malda in 1866, says, "In the south
district, throughout the whole tract of country, the Bamboo
has flowered, and the seed has been sold in the bazaar at
thirteen seers (26 lbs.) for three rupees, rice being ten seers,
the ryots having stored enough for their own wants in
addition. Hundreds of maunds (the maund being 100 lbs.)
have been sold in the English bazaar at Malda, and large
quantities have been sent to Sultangunge and other places
25 to 30 miles distant, showing how enormous the supply
must have been." Mr. Gray adds, "The Bamboo harvest
has been quite providential, as the ryots were on the
point of starving."[1] Sir Joseph Hooker in his *Himalayan
Journals*, p. 107 (ed. 1891) says: "The young shoots of
several (Bamboos) are eaten, and the seeds of one are made
into a fermented drink, and into bread in times of scarcity;
but it would take many pages to describe the numerous
purposes to which the various species are put." His account
of the ingenious way in which his Lepcha servants used to
improvise huts and furniture on his travels in little more
than an hour, with no handier tool than a long knife, is most
curious and interesting. Near the top of a pass from the
Teesta to the great Rungeet he found "a plant of Praong (a
small Bamboo) in full seed; this sends up many flowering
branches from the root and but few leaf-bearing ones, and
after maturing its seed and giving off suckers from the root,
the parent plant dies. The fruit is a dark, long grain, like
Rice; it is boiled and made into cakes, or into beer like
Murwa" (*Ib.* p. 220).

[1] Munro, p. 4.

To the Chinaman, as to the Japanese, the Bamboo is of supreme value; indeed, it may be said that there is not a necessity, a luxury, or a pleasure of his daily life to which it does not minister. It furnishes the framework of his house and thatches the roof over his head, while it supplies paper for his windows, awnings for his sheds, and blinds for his verandah. His beds, his tables, his chairs, his cupboards, his thousand and one small articles of furniture are made of it. Shavings and shreds of Bamboos are used to stuff his pillows and his mattresses. The retail dealer's measures, the carpenter's rule, the farmer's water-wheel and irrigating pipes, cages for birds, crickets, and other pets, vessels of all kinds, from the richly lacquered flower-stands of the well-to-do gentleman down to the humblest utensils, the wretchedest duds of the very poor, all come from the same source. The boatman's raft, and the pole with which he punts it along; his ropes, his mat-sails, and the ribs to which they are fastened; the palanquin in which the stately mandarin is borne to his office, the bride to her wedding, the coffin to the grave; the cruel instruments of the executioner, the lazy painted beauty's fan and parasol, the soldier's spear, quiver, and arrows, the scribe's pen, the student's book, the artist's brush and the favourite study for his sketch; the musician's flute, mouth-organ, plectrum, and a dozen various instruments of strange shapes and still stranger sounds—in the making of all these the Bamboo is a first necessity. Plaiting and wicker-work of all kinds, from the coarsest baskets and matting down to the delicate filagree with which porcelain cups are encased—so cunningly that it would seem as if no fingers less deft than those of fairies

could have woven the dainty web—are a common and
obvious use of the fibre. The same material made into great
hats like inverted baskets protects the coolie from the sun,
while the labourers in the rice fields go about looking like
animated haycocks in waterproof coats made of the dried
leaves of Bamboo sewn together. See at the corner of the
street a fortune-teller attracting a crowd around him as he
tells the future by the aid of slips of Bamboo graven with
mysterious characters and shaken up in a Bamboo cup, and
every man around him smoking a Bamboo pipe. See in
yonder cook-shop the son of Han regaling himself with a
mess of Bamboo shoots, which have been cooked in a vessel
of the same material coated with clay, and are eaten with
chopsticks which may have grown on the same parent stem.
Such shoots, either in the shape of pickles or preserved in
sugar, are an article of export from south to north where
they are esteemed a delicacy.

Then there is the famous medicine Tabashir, the great
and infallible nostrum with which some Buddhist priest or
Chinese Dulcamara will promise to heal you of every and
any ailment. In certain Bamboos, especially, according to
Roxburgh, in the Melocanna bambusoides, there is found in
the cavities between the knots a substance consisting of
silica with a little lime and vegetable matter, or sometimes
of silica and potash in the proportion of about seventy parts
of silica to thirty of potash. It is said to be formed by
extravasation of the juices of the plant in consequence of
some diseased condition of the nodes or joints. Beautifully
opalescent, the loveliness of Tabashir is by the faithful
regarded as only equalled by its medicinal virtues. Some

idea of the quantity of silica contained in Bamboos may be gathered from the fact recorded that one species, Bambusa Tabacaria, will emit sparks when struck with an axe.

House, furniture, art, clothes, arms, food, and medicine, what does this wonderful plant not supply? And it is all so cheap, too ; for the materials of a common dwelling-house in the south of China cost about twenty-five dollars ![1]

Near the Malay villages, where the houses are carried upon poles above the red teeming swamp, like the old lacustrine dwellings, there is sure to be a Bamboo grove. Towards evening, when the fresh sea-borne breeze drives the burning stillness of the day before it, bringing to the poor washed-out natives a faint renewal of energy, weird and ghostly strains come floating upon the air. It is no mortal music, for Æolus himself is the musician, rivalling the great god Pan of old. In one of the hollow stems of the grove holes have been pierced, some greater and some less, one in each joint ; through these the Wind-God breathes fitful wailing sounds, now deep like the pedal notes of an organ, now soft as a fairy's flute. This is Bulu Perindu, the plaintive Bamboo, the analogue of the Æolian harp.[2]

Strange to say, the Bamboo played an important, though, fortunately, inconspicuous, part in the history of European industry. In the sixth century, when Justinian was reigning at Constantinople, the court reserved to itself a monopoly of the silk trade and of its manufacture, the looms being worked by women in the Imperial Palace. Up to that time the silkworms that feed upon the leaves of the white

[1] Compare Williams's *Middle Kingdom*, vol. i. p. 360.
[2] Compare Sir Emerson Tennant's *Ceylon*, vol. i.; Munro, p. 2.

Mulberry were confined to China; those which haunt the
Pine, the Oak, and the Ash were common in the forests both
of Asia and Europe, but as their education is more difficult
and their produce more uncertain, they were generally
neglected, except in the little island of Ceos, near the coast
of Attica. The Persians had the monopoly of the trade in
Chinese silk. This was a matter of deep concern to
Justinian, who endeavoured to procure the raw material for
his looms through his adventurous Christian allies, the
Abyssinians, who at that time were a naval and commercial
power. His negotiations failed, the Abyssinians declining a
competition with the Persians, whose proximity to India
must give them an overwhelming advantage. Another
expedient, however, presented itself. Two Persian monks,
who had long been resident in China, travelled to Constantinople, a giant's journey, and proposed to the Emperor that
they should endeavour to introduce the eggs of the silkworm
into Europe. The offer was accepted and liberally encouraged
by Justinian. The two monks returned to China, and by
smuggling the eggs in the hollow of a cane contrived to
elude the vigilance of the Chinese, and made their way
safely to Constantinople with their precious treasure. It is
not too much to say that in that fragment of Bamboo were
carried the future commercial fortunes of Lyons, of Genoa,
of Spitalfields, and all the other great manufactories of
Europe, for from those eggs were descended all the races
and varieties which stocked the Western World. But the
pity of it is that we have not the record of the travels and
adventures of those two Persian monks! This memorable
importation is assigned to the year 552 A.D. (Gibbon,

Decline and Fall of the Roman Empire, chap. xl.; *Encyclo-pædia Britannica*, Article, " Silk ").

There is one use which I would not recommend. One day in the north of China I was calling upon a French friend. I found him in his garden with a large gang of coolies, superintending the laying out of some new shrubberies and flower-beds. Knowing him to be ignorant of the language, I expressed my astonishment, and asked him how he managed to make them understand. "Ah! mon cher," said the little man, shaking his cane viciously, " J'ai ici le meilleur interprète du monde —le Professeur Bambou." Like some other interpreters, the Bamboo is apt in that capacity to lead to trouble.

It is to be regretted that, however well we may succeed in the cultivation of Bamboos for pleasure and ornament, the plant which is so rich in economic value in its own country is not likely to prove useful here. I consulted a leading London umbrella and stick maker on the subject, and he told me that in his trade they were obliged even to eschew the canes of the South of France as insufficiently ripened, and consequently liable to split. It would seem, then, that we must be contented with the beauty of our plants and ask no more of them than they can give; but it is hard to think that out of so much wealth we cannot even achieve the humble triumph of an umbrella stick.

In his *Note sur la culture du Bambou et ses usages industriels dans la région des Pyrénées et dans le sudouest de la France* (1878) M. Calvert, sub-inspector of forests, gives some interesting particulars as to the success which has attended the venture started by M. Guillemin in 1861 at Gan in the Basses Pyrénées.

D

At that date the area under Bamboo cultivation was a slope of 4 hectares, or rather more than 9 acres, 350 mètres above sea-level. The cost of planting was 3000 francs per acre. The plants reached maturity in from seven to eight years, at the end of which period the older shoots were removed for industrial purposes, bringing in a profit of from 800 to 1000 francs per hectare annually. ·

The species recommended for cultivation are NIGRA, used for umbrella sticks, sword canes, whip handles, fishing-rods, and various purposes; MITIS, used for the same purposes as NIGRA, the rhizomes being used also for cups, napkin rings, egg-cups, goads for oxen, sticks for beating walnut and chestnut trees, etc.; and MÉTAKÉ, of which are made pipe-stems, cigar and cigarette tubes, pen and pencil-holders, bird-calls, and other objects.

He gives the following list of objects with the prices actually obtained at Gan :—

	Francs.
Bundles of bamboos in the rough for whip handles without roots	50·00 per hundred
Bundles dressed with roots	18·00 per dozen
Parcels of bamboo whips with roots . .	60·00 „
„ „ without roots . .	48·00 „
Fishing-rods with top joints	0·50 per mètre
Spare top joints according to length from 30 to	50·00 per hundred
Bundles of bamboos for umbrellas in the rough	10·00 „
„ „ „ dressed .	100·00 „
Alpine sticks for tourists without roots . .	18·00 per dozen
„ „ with roots . .	24·00 „
Ox-goads with spring point	12·00 „
„ mounted with iron	15·00 „
Handles for caterpillar destroyers . . .	0·25 per mètre
Handles for extinguishers used in churches .	0·25 „
„ „ „ for gas . .	0·30 „
Quoin sticks and frames	0·25 „

	Francs.	
Drinking cups	3·00	per dozen
Napkin rings	1·50	,,
Egg-cups	1·50	,,
Paper-cutters . . . . . ,	3·00	,,
Shoe-horns	3·00	,,
Tobacco pipes made of bamboo roots, prices varying	. from 3 to 10·00 each	
Paper made of stems and leaves of bamboo .	No price given	
Inkstands	3·00 per dozen	
Penholders in the rough	2·00 per hundred	
Stems of bamboo fit for paper-making . .	No price given	
Canes known as "Java" (? Wang-hai) made of rhizomes	} from 2 to 5 each	
Canes known as "Queues de mulet" made of the rhizomes which shoot up above ground		

M. Calvert further notes the value of Bamboos for binding together with their rhizomes movable soil on sloping ground, a merit also pointed out by Messrs. Rivière in their monograph.

The economical results obtained at Gan might perhaps tempt some enterprising horticulturist or farmer in Devonshire or Cornwall to make an experiment of a similar nature. The cultivation of Bamboos is of the easiest; the plants renew themselves, new shoots taking the place of those which are cut; and a permanent profit of something like £16 per acre at the end of eight years is an alluring bait. But it must be remembered that since 1878 means of communication with the far East have vastly increased ; Bamboo canes are imported at a very low rate, and those ripened under a tropical or sub-tropical sun are, as I have already pointed out, tougher and more reliable than those even of the South of France.

Tough indeed the canes must be that are to make the frames of bicycles and tricycles. A report in one of the daily newspapers of a recent show of cycles says, "No one would credit, until after actual trial, the strength and rigidity which the bamboo cycles possess, coupled at the same time with a definite amount of increased comfort."

The latest honour achieved by a Bamboo is (according to a Birmingham paper) that of having furnished to a church in Shanghai a set of organ pipes which, for softness and mellowness of tone, outdo all others.

In the superstitions of the world the Bamboo has its place. Rumpf, who died in the year 1693, says, in his *Herbarium Amboinense*, that the Malays in his time believed that the first man sprang from the hollow stem of the Bamboo. The Garrows, a race inhabiting the western extremity of the mountain range at the bend of the Burrampooter, whom Sir Joseph Hooker describes in his *Himalayan Journals* as a savage race, given to human sacrifices and polyandry, are said by De Gubernatis in his *Mythologie des Plantes* to have neither temple nor altar. They erect before their huts a pillar of Bamboo, which they decorate with flowers and cotton and offer up sacrifice to the divinity in front of it.

In some Eastern countries the rarely recurrent flowering of the Bamboos is regarded as a sure presage of great calamity. The *North Borneo Herald* of 1st August 1894 has a paragraph upon the subject in connection with the terrible visitation of the plague which ravaged Hong-Kong in 1894.

THE BLOOM ON THE BAMBOO

A Hong-Kong paper has the following note : The bloom on the Bamboo has indeed proved an unerring portent of evil in this year of disaster. It is well known as a rare phenomenon in the botanical world, and is always in the Oriental mind associated with impending

calamity. After the Bamboo in the spring had flowered to an
abnormal degree it was confidently predicted by the superstitious
native that much evil was about to fall upon us. Unfortunately,
only too true was the presentiment, for during many decades no more
serious blow has fallen on the prosperity and happiness of the colony
than the plague which manifested itself just as the swaying Bamboos
burst into verdancy. Of course, it is quite possible that there is
more in the belief that the flowering cane means ill than we might
at first imagine. Such a phenomenon is doubtless due to abnormal
atmospheric and climatic conditions, which, while causing the Bamboos
to flower, may be also fertile to the development of various diseases.
The index may therefore be more or less reliable, as reliable indeed
as the data on which we foretell the weather.

The editor of the Hong-Kong paper might have added
the Chinese-Japanese war as another disastrous sequel to
the portent.

In the gay decorations with which the holiday-loving
Japanese brighten their houses and streets in honour of the
new year the Bamboo is a conspicuous feature. On the
28th or 29th day of the twelfth month the work of decoration
begins. A Fir tree and a stem of Bamboo are planted on
either side of the principal door of the house, and between
them is hung a cord of straw. To this cord are suspended
a boiled lobster, a piece of charcoal, a large Orange, a dried
Persimmon,[1] a frond of Bracken, a leaf of the evergreen Oak,
and a piece of seaweed, all tied together into a sort of
bouquet. The Fir and the Bamboo are evergreen emblems
of long life ; the lobster, strong in spite of its crooked back,
is an emblem of bent, but hale old age ; the charcoal, which
does not decay, represents imperishability ; the Orange, from
its name, Dai-dai, which by a pun means "from generation
to generation," and from the fact of its being supposed to

[1] The fruit of Diospyrus Kaki.

hang longer on the tree than any other fruit, is in like
manner of auspicious omen; the dried Persimmon, which
long preserves its taste, represents the unchanged sweetness
of conjugal love and fidelity; the Bracken is held to be slow
in fading; the Oak leaf does not fall off the tree until the
young leaf is ready to take its place, just as a father is
happy who does not die until his son is fit to succeed him;
while the seaweed, Kompu or Kobu, composes the last two
syllables of *yorokobu*, "to be happy." The rope of straw
represents the rope which the gods, after they had lured out
the sun-goddess, according to the myth which in the Shinto
religion springs from the first eclipse of the sun, hung
outside the stone cave of heaven in order to prevent her
from returning into it. These various emblems are hung
up to propitiate the Year-God, praying him to preserve the
house from evil during the ensuing twelve months. They
are taken down on the seventh day of the first month, and
on the fourteenth day they are burnt in honour of Sai no
Kami, the god of roads and protector of travellers. The
origin of this custom is lost in antiquity. It is alluded to in
the collection of poems called the "Hundred Heads," compiled
by the Emperor Horikawa at the end of the eleventh century,
where, in the poem by one of the nobles of the court named
Akisuyé, is found the following passage: "When the Fir
trees are placed at the doors we know that the night will
break into the morning of the new year." Such customs
do not grow in a day; so it is fair to suppose that this one
was already of respectable age 800 years ago.

CHAPTER V

Etymology

PROBABLY the first European author in whose writings any allusion is to be found to the giant Grasses is Ctesias, who has a story of Indian canes big enough to be used as boats. Colonel Yule brands this as one of the writer's "biggest bounces." No doubt Ctesias did often draw a very long bow. But then it must be remembered that he never was in India, and that his book was based upon hearsay picked up at the Court of Persia four hundred years B.C., when he was private physician to King Artaxerxes Mnemon.

Colonel Yule's article on the word Bamboo in his *Glossary of Anglo-Indian Words* (J. Murray, 1886) is most interesting and curious. It would seem as if it were fated that some mystery should enshroud everything connected with these plants. Their very name is as great a puzzle to etymologists as their different species are a riddle to botanists. The word Bamboo, says Colonel Yule,

One of the commonest in Anglo-Indian daily use, and thoroughly naturalised in English, is of exceedingly obscure origin. According to Wilson, it is Canarese Banbu. Marsden inserts it in his dictionary as good Malay. Crawfurd says it is certainly used on the west coast

of Sumatra as a native word, but that it is elsewhere unknown to the
Malay language. The usual Malay word is Buluh. He thinks it
more likely to have found its way into English from Sumatra than
from Canara. But there is evidence enough of its familiarity among
the Portuguese before the end of the sixteenth century to indicate
the probability that we adopted the word, like so many others,
through them. We believe that the correct Canarese word is Banwu.
In the sixteenth century the word in the Concan appears to have been
Mambu, or at least so it was represented by the Portuguese.
Rumphius seems to suggest a quaint onomatopœia: "Vehementissimos
edunt ictus et sonitus, quum incendio comburuntur, quando notum ejus
nomen Bambu, Basubu, facile exauditur" (*Herbarium Amboinense,*
iv. 17). It is possible that the Canarese word is a vernacular
corruption or development of the Sanskrit Vansa. Bamboo does not
occur, so far as we can find, in any of the earlier sixteenth century
books, which employ Canna or the like.

Colonel Yule quotes passages from many of the old
writers illustrating the first use of the word. Three extracts
will be curious and suffice for our purpose. Garcia, in his
*Colloquois dos Simples e Drogas e cousas Medecinaes da
India,* published in 1563, says, speaking of Tabashir, the
drug extracted from the canes of Bamboos, "The people from
whom it is got call it sacar-mambum . . . because the
canes of that plant are called by the Indians Mambu."

The two following passages are from Acosta's *Tractulo
de las Drogas y Medecinas de las Indias Orientales.* 4to.
Burgos, 1578:—

Some of these (canes), especially in Malabar, are found so large
that the people make use of them as boats, not opening them out, but
cutting one of the canes right across and using the natural knots to
stop the ends, and so a couple of naked blacks go upon it . . .
each of them at his own end of the Mambu (so they call it) being
provided with two paddles, one in each hand . . . and so upon
a cane of this kind the folk pass across, and sitting with their legs
clinging naked.

Again :—

And many people on that river (of Cranganor) made use of these canes in place of boats, to be safe from the numerous crocodiles or caymoins (as they call them) which are in the river (which are in fact great and ferocious lizards).

Colonel Yule accepts these passages as " explaining, if not justifying," the "big bounce" of Ctesias. The two earliest quotations cited by Colonel Yule in which the name appears in its present form are Fitch, in Hakluyt, ii. 391 (A.D. 1586): "All the houses are made of canes, which they call Bambos, and bee covered with straw"; and Linschoten (printed at London by John Wolfe, 1598), "A thicke reede as big as a man's legge, which is called Bambus."

Classification

Munro divides the Bambusaceæ into three sections :—

1. TRIGLOSSÆ, which have three stamens and spiculæ, with two or three bracts at the base.

2. BAMBUSEÆ VERÆ.—True Bamboos, which have six stamens and several bracts.

3. BACCIFERÆ, which have six stamens, several bracts, and berry or apple-shaped fruit.

The Triglossæ are sub-divided again into three sub-sections :—

1. ARUNDINARLÆ.

2. ARTHROSTYLIDEÆ.

3. CHUSQUEÆ.

The first sub-section (Arundinariæ) contains three groups:—

(1) ARUNDINARIA.

(2) THAMNOCALAMUS.

(3) PHYLLOSTACHYS.

To one or other of these three groups of the sub-section Arundinariæ it is probable that almost, if not quite, all of the hardy Bamboos must be referred, though Munro classes some of them with which he was imperfectly acquainted, not having seen the flowers, as Bambuseæ veræ. Where a doubt exists as to the classification of a species it is perhaps better to preserve the familiar style Bambusa; it being clearly understood that this is done without prejudice, and does not imply a declaration of faith that the plant so named belongs to the Bambuseæ veræ of science.

For gardening purposes the Bamboos have been separated into two divisions :—

1. Those which in their own country come into growth in the summer.

2. Those which show their shoots in the spring.

With the former division we have nothing to do. They are aliens that cannot support themselves, and there is no home for them in England. The latter, on the contrary, we may receive with open arms and gladly adopt as most useful, naturalised subjects. It must be obvious that plants which renew their life so late in the year that it needs the full power of a scorching climate to enable them to ripen their wood, must starve under the feeble and uncertain rays of our sun. Those, on the other hand, which in their own home begin to grow in spring, though some of them are later here, can mature their new shoots in time for them to ripen before winter.

On the 8th of April 1894 I found shoots from 6 inches to 1 foot long on plants of Phyllostachys aurea, viridi-glaucescens, Henonis, nigra, and nigro-punctata; they proved, however, to be by no means the most vigorous growths of the year on the same plants. They were on specimens planted in the late autumn of 1891 (as I now know, the worst period that could have been chosen for open-air planting), and the growth showed itself far earlier than it had done in the two previous years. The last species of Phyllostachys to give signs of life in each year has been P. mitis, a very recalcitrant Bamboo so far as my observation goes. I have some plants of this species which, although showing no appearance of weakening, have not yet, in the third summer of their existence here, put forth a single new shoot. Others made good growth during their first summer, none during the second, and are now again pushing vigorously. Others, again, which grew in the second summer are idle this year; some have made growth each year. When the growth does come, patience is rewarded. It is so rapid that it has plenty of time to mature its stems, with the exception, indeed, of a few belated laggards which are foredoomed. The larger Arundinarias, especially Simoni as we shall see later on, lose many autumn shoots in this way. Still the great mass of the shoots of the spring-growing species may be relied upon, and seeing that by degrees, as the plants become established in their new home, they season by season put forth their young growth earlier, the complete acclimatisation even of such lazy colonists as Phyllostachys mitis would seem to be only a question of time and patience.

It is to China and Japan, that inexhaustible source which for thirty years has been continuously pouring new treasures into our gardens and parks, that we owe most of our hardy Bamboos. So far India has only yielded us five species capable of cultivation in the open air in our country, and

indeed one of these, Thamnocalamus Falconeri, can scarcely
be called hardy, though it flourishes in Cornwall and in
Ireland. From the United States of North America we draw
one species, Arundinaria macrosperma. The Andes (unless,
indeed, Bambusa disticha should prove to be identical with
Chusquea tessellata) and Africa have hitherto given us
nothing. I shall call attention to their possibilities later on.

The botanical distinctions between the inflorescence of
the two genera Thamnocalamus and Arundinaria are so
slight, that it seems probable that the two will ultimately
be merged in one. But between these and the Bamboos of
the Phyllostachys group the differences are great and strike
the eye at once, and it is, therefore, important to point them
out. Leaving to skilled botanists the task of lifting the veil
which still enshrouds the mysteries of flower and fruit, it
may be said roughly that the main and more easily observable
characteristics of the two sections are as follows :—

In Arundinaria the stems are straight and round, the
branches are partially verticillate, that is to say, they
seem to nearly encircle the stem, and they appear almost
simultaneously along the whole length of the cane as soon
as its full growth has been attained, and not before. If
anything, the lower branches are rather behind the middle
and upper ones.

In Phyllostachys, on the contrary, the branches begin to
open out at the lower end of the stem a little while before
the full growth in height has been attained, and gradually
develop themselves upwards. The internode or merithal on
the side on which the branches spring is grooved or
channelled owing to the pressure of the branches (of which

there are generally two, or at most three, in which latter
case one drops off), which, being closely packed under the
sheaths against the cane while it is in a soft state, leave a
permanent double furrow on the internode, and the cane
itself is more or less, sometimes almost imperceptibly,
zigzagged from joint to joint.   Of the two persistent
branches one is always much longer than the other.   As a
rule, the sheaths which protect the branches in their embryo
state are far more persistent in the Arundinaria than in the
Phyllostachys, their dead appearance being a sore disfigure-
ment to some species, as, for instance, in Arundinaria
japonica (Métaké) and Arundinaria Simoni.   In the Phyllostachys the sheaths drop as soon as the branches spring
away at an angle from the side of the stem, while in the
Arundinaria they are apt to bend back with the branches
and remain encircling them, furnishing them with a comfortable jacket until they are able to take care of themselves.
Then, and not till then, they fall off.

Many of the Arundinarias have those portions of the
internodes which are not encased in the sheaths covered by a
thick, waxy, white secretion like the bloom on a purple grape,
contrasting finely with the green colour of the stem.   This is
very noticeable in Arundinaria nitida, Arundinaria Hindsii,
and others.   This waxy bloom in plants serves a distinct and
important purpose in preventing the stomata, or mouths which
are the organs of transpiration, from becoming stopped with
water either in the shape of rain or dew.   In the leaves of
Bamboos there is another provision for protecting the
stomata in the shape of solid peg-like projections of the
cuticle—of course, both the stomata and their protections are

only visible under the microscope. An illustration of a vertical section of a Bamboo leaf magnified 180 diameters is given at page 296 of Part III. of Kerner and Oliver's *Natural History of Plants*, together with parts of the same section magnified 460 diameters : this illustration clearly shows the whole mechanism. But the same authors describe a very simple experiment by which its effect may be seen.

On plunging a bamboo leaf in water a surprising sight presents itself. The upper side, covered by a dark green, smooth, flat epidermis, with no stomata, becomes wet all over and retains its dark colour and dull appearance ; but the under surface, blue green in colour, and beset with stomata and thousands of cuticular pegs, does not allow the air to be displaced, and this layer of air, spread thin over the surface, glistens under water like polished silver ! The leaf may be shaken under water to any extent, and may even be left submerged for a week, but the silvery glistening air stratum is not dislodged. If such a leaf is now taken out of the water, the upper surface is quite wet, but the under surface is dry, like a hand which has been dipped in mercury and then withdrawn, and not the smallest drop of water adheres to it. On placing a vessel of water, in which some bamboo leaves are half immersed, under the receiver of an air-pump and then pumping out the air, numerous small air-bubbles are at once given off from the submerged portions of the leaves. At length the silvery lustre disappears, and the air between the cuticular pegs is replaced by water. If now the leaves be completely submerged, the silver lustre is only shown on those parts which were not previously immersed, and where water could not replace the exhausted air,—the spaces round the pegs in this region having been again supplied with air on the opening of the stopcock of the pump in order to submerge the leaves. It may be imagined from this experiment how much the stomata would be damaged by water if the plants mentioned were not protected from moisture by the pegs to which the air adheres so strongly.

A third contrivance of Nature for guarding the stomata of plants against excessive wet is to be found in " the hair-like structures which interlace and form a loose felt work." This is very noticeable, even without a lens, especially on the under side of many of the Bamboo leaves, for example in Arundinaria auricoma. But those who are curious upon the subject must go for further information to the fountain-head from which I have quoted.

The waxy bloom is especially thick immediately below the projecting nodes of certain Arundinarias, to wit Arundinaria Simoni; from which it would seem that for structural reasons there is more danger of the stomata being choked by the rising dew than by the falling rain, that is to say, either that they are more numerous immediately under than immediately above the node, or that the lower part, not being protected at an early stage by the sheaths which spring from and encircle the upper node, need this extra defence.

In the very differently constructed plants of the Phyllostachys group, such as P. mitis, P. aurea, P. nigra, P. viridi-glaucescens, there is no hairy down to be found on the stems, and the bloom is only seen sparsely scattered immediately below the nodes. Probably their hard, compact, and almost flinty epidermis does not stand in need of any protection, the stomata, or transpiratory organs being situated on the under side of the leaves.[1]

Again, in Arundinaria the axillary buds of the branches,

---

[1] Some idea of the vast numbers of these stomata may be given by the statement that on the under side of an Oak leaf no less than 2 millions of stomata have been found, while in the Water Lily leaf they reach 11½ millions ! In succulent plants, such as the House-leek and the Stone-crop, there are very few stomata, only from 10 to 20 in one square millimeter, which in the majority of plants would show from 200 to 300.—Kerner and Oliver, Part III., pp. 281, 288.

which are the future branchlets, are out of sight, imprisoned closely as in a strait-waistcoat by the sheaths which clasp the stems so tightly that until they fall aside of themselves you can hardly strip them off by force. In Phyllostachys the sheaths of the branchlets are developed from the outer scale of the conspicuous bud; and this bud is of no small use in helping us to identify the very inconveniently similar species, for in each member of the family it has a distinct character. In the early spring, before the plants have begun to put forth new leaves, in the axils of the ramification are to be seen the brilliant, richly-enamelled, scaly buds, which the summer will develop into new branches, beginning to swell. A careful observer will then at once be able to recognise the variations between the different sorts. In P. mitis, for instance, the glaze is of a purplish brown, strongly marked; in P. aurea it is somewhat variable, but pale in colour. Quilioi has the base of the bud green and only the tip is brown. Flexuosa has a rather dark brownish pink bud; while in P. viridi-glaucescens it is a pale green. The buds of P. nigra and nigro-punctata are brown mottled with black, whereas those of Boryana are fair in colour, almost belying its reputed close relationship to the two latter. Henonis has a pale yellowish green bud. In every instance the bud seems to be strongly characteristic of the Bamboo. So much for the general distinctions between the two great groups of Hardy Bamboos.

Almost all the Bamboos which are hardy in this country, grow like Couch Grass from rhizomes or creeping rootstocks. Some of our Bamboos, such as Arundinaria Simoni, Arundinaria japonica (Métaké), Arundinaria Veitchii, Bambusa pygmæa, Phyllostachys viridi-glaucescens, Phyllostachys violescens,

Bambusa palmata, and others, have strong running roots invading everything, and therefore demand well-isolated positions. Others, such as Phyllostachys mitis, and more especially Phyllostachys aurea, seem, under the cramping conditions of our soil and climate, to lose their power of spreading. It will be better to consider these features when we come to the descriptions of the various species ; it may, however, be said here that it is not for some years, not indeed until stout growth has been made, that root action takes place in earnest. This observation does not apply to such sturdy travellers as Arundinaria Simoni, Arundinaria pygmæa, or Arundinaria Veitchii, which it is difficult to keep within bounds at any stage of their existence ; but plants of Arundinaria japonica (Métaké), some 11 feet high and a couple of yards or more in diameter, which have been established in my garden for seven years, are only just beginning to throw up shoots at some distance from the parent stems.

Some idea of the vigour with which the Bamboos spread in their native homes may be formed from the following remark of Professor Sargent in his *Forest Flora of Japan*, p. 7 :—

In Japan the forest-floor is covered, even high on the mountains and in the extreme north, with a continuous, almost impenetrable, mass of dwarf Bamboos of several species, which makes travelling in the woods, except over long beaten paths and up the beds of streams, practically impossible. These Bamboos, which vary in height from 3 to 6 feet in different parts of the country, make the forest-floor monotonous and uninteresting, and prevent the growth of nearly all other under-shrubs, except the most vigorous species. Shrubs therefore are mostly driven to the borders of roads and other open places, or to the banks of streams and lakes, where they can obtain sufficient light to enable them to rise above the Bamboos ; and it is the abundance of the Bamboo, no doubt, which has developed the

E

climbing habit of many Japanese plants, which are obliged to ascend the trees in search of sun and light, for the Japanese forest is filled with climbing shrubs, which flourish with tropical luxuriance.

Truly a startling statement!

Occasionally it happens in Bamboo groves that a rhizome in its subterranean travels will meet with some obstacle such as a stone; immediately it grows upwards and forms an arch over the barrier, often rising above ground for the purpose of escaping from it, and then, curving down again, it plunges into the ground once more to continue its underground course.   Beware of carrying a gun at full cock through a Bamboo grove!   In countries where Bamboos are planted in carefully-prepared beds this phenomenon will be rarely seen.   But I have one well-defined example of it in a clump of Phyllostachys nigra, and others in clumps of Bambusa palmata, where the rhizomes have formed distinct hoops above ground in order to avoid a stone or stump which barred their progress.

The direction followed by the creeping rootstocks of Bamboos is a straight line from the parent stem.   Such a line may be traced for some yards in the case of Arundinaria Simoni by the stems which spring from the knots of the rhizome.   These stems throw out roots downwards as will be seen presently, forming, as it were, separate plants, from which in turn rhizomes will be sent forth in every direction. The depth of the root varies in different species.   In the case of Arundinaria Simoni they have been found buried more than a yard from the surface.   Even the tiny A. pygmæa, which in proportion to its size is the greatest wanderer of all its tribe in this country, will send its roots down some 2 feet.

The underground growth of the Bamboo may be well understood by examining one of the flexible Wang-hai canes sold by whip and stick makers. These canes are indeed made of the rhizomes or creeping rootstocks of Phyllostachys (probably P. nigra). In one now before me the knots are from 1 inch to 2 inches apart; the internodes are fistulous, though the pipe is very narrow, only one-sixteenth of an inch in diameter. The pipe is, of course, sealed by the septum at each node. All round the knots are the scars left by cutting away the verticillated rootlets, and on each knot, placed alternately, is a larger scar marking the place once occupied by the stem-bud. From this scar there runs along the internode an indented channel or groove, which becomes gradually shallower until it dies away in the next knot. The internode is deeply depressed in the centre.[1]

The birth of the bud is the point upon which the chief interest is concentrated. As has been shown above, it springs from a node of the creeping rootstock. It first appears as a small hard cone safely encased in an armour of protecting sheaths. When vegetation begins to take place it softens and swells until it has grown far larger in bulk than the underground stem which bears it. As it grows it is drawn up telescope-wise until two or three tiny green blades, sometimes brown, sometimes yellowish or striped, are seen piercing the surface of the soil. Almost at the same time roots begin to strike downwards from the base of the rising cane and a new plant asserts its independence.

Watch a plant of Phyllostachys mitis. Slowly, very

[1] The underground stem of an Arundinaria, which presents certain variations from that of Phyllostachys, will be found described under Arundinaria Simoni, p. 63.

slowly at first, the cone pushes its way through the top of the
soil. For a day or two, indeed, nothing is seen but the little
tongues which are the tongue-like blades of the two or three
topmost sheaths. By degrees a little more of the stem
appears, but the growth is very deliberate, as if the newly-
born baby were taking careful note of its surroundings and
making up its mind whether it be worth while to play a part
in so doubtful a world. Sometimes, indeed, it decides to
make no further effort. Of two or three, to all appearance,
equally healthy shoots on the same plant one will often,
without rhyme or reason, fade away during this hesitating
period of almost arrested growth. Its mates, on the contrary,
after a while begin to push forward vigorously and to show
their true character. The shoots are round, fat, and pointed,
closely packed in the alternate sheaths which, each surmounted by its little ligule and blade, spring from what will
presently appear as the joints of the cane. The function of
the ligule, which adheres closely to the stem, is to prevent
water in the shape of rain from running down and choking the
stomata of the bud. Sometimes it is grooved so as to make
channels, and often it is fringed with hairs, curling so as to
direct the downward course of the water. Gradually the growth
becomes faster until the culm has attained about two-thirds
of its height, when it begins to slacken, until at last it is
almost imperceptible. When the shoot has grown to nearly
its full height,[1] the lower sheaths begin to stand out from the
stem and the branches first show themselves. This process
continues upwards until the topmost branch has been revealed,

---

[1] According to Messrs. Rivière, the branching occurs much earlier in the
life of the stem. Difference of climate may account for this.

and the sheaths, having played their part as protectors and being no longer wanted, drop off. At first they adhere to the internode so closely that you cannot tear them apart. When they are gone, the channelling of the stem on the side on which the branchlets grow is distinctly visible. Soon the leaves appear, and the plant is arrayed in all its beauty. As the wood ripens its texture becomes more compact and the circumference contracts. In some six weeks the culm has grown to its full size. Neither in height nor in bulk will succeeding years add aught to it; branches and foliage will be more dense, and the rootstock will grow until the plant has reached its utmost capabilities. Next year's stems will be taller and stouter; their elder brother may grow no more.

In the Arundinarias, as has been already remarked, the growth is different. The sheaths do not begin to loosen their hold in order to make way for the growth of the branchlets until the full height of the culm has been attained. The ramification is almost simultaneous throughout the length of the cane, though the upper branches often are a little ahead of the others. In fact, the development is downwards, rather than upwards as it is in the Phyllostachoides. The sheaths often do not drop off until the second year.

One phenomenon described by Messrs. Rivière in the early life of the canes is so wonderful that I cannot but note it. In Algiers every year at the moment when the buds are formed, particularly in the cases of Bambusa macroculmis, B. Hookeri, B. vulgaris, and Phyllostachys mitis, the soil is hardened by the long droughts peculiar to the climate; but round the plants the earth begins to show signs of moisture, gradually the surface heaves and cracks, and with this mysterious assistance the shoots are enabled to push upwards. A careful examination for two or three days after the first appearance, especially in the early morning, shows that during the night the bud has supplied or condensed a quantity of water sufficient to soak the earth by which it is surrounded. The bud itself at early dawn, before sunrise, is abundantly impregnated with moisture. How is this moisture produced? Perhaps it comes from a secretion of the plant, for on its young and hardly-developed organs there appear tiny drops which from time to time are detached and fall upon the soil. At first it was supposed that this moisture, which was observed every morning, might be caused by the condensation of night dews or mists upon the young shoots; but where these had been covered and protected against all external influences the same phenomena were observed. Various and repeated experiments failed to give any definite explanation of the cause of this moisture. In the month of August 1874 Messrs. Rivière observed what they describe as showers of rain falling from the leaves of certain Bamboos at eventide. They were enabled to gather enough of this water to take its temperature. Whether the former wonder occurs here, even in a modified degree, I am unable to say, for our plants are so heavily mulched that it would scarcely be possible to observe it, but I certainly have noticed dewdrops standing on the leaves and stems of my Bamboos when the surrounding vegetation, both above, below, and at the same height, was quite dry.

There is one feature which I have observed in the hardy Bamboos, and which, as it is constant, I desire to record.

All those Bamboos, without a single exception, which have been proved to be thoroughly hardy in this climate have the veins of their leaves tessellated, that is to say, in chequers, crossing one another like the threads of a spider's web or the meshes of a net. All those which have been relegated to the temperate house as tender or only half-hardy have the veins of their leaves striated, that is to say, running in parallel lines from the base to the point. This characteristic may be seen with the naked eye by holding the leaf up to the light, but with a lens it is very distinct. Let me give instances. Of the Himalayan species up to the present in cultivation, Thamnocalamus Falconeri and Arundinaria falcata die down in winter, the latter, indeed, does so in its own country ; their leaf veins are striated. Arundinaria race-mosa, A. aristata, and Thamnocalamus spathiflorus are quite hardy ; their leaf veins are tessellated. Out of some forty Japanese species which I have tried, two only, namely, Suo-chiku (Bambusa Alphonse Karri of the French) and Taiho-chiku (B. vittata argentea), are very tender and not to be trusted ; their leaf veins are striated.

It would be, of course, idle to assert that every Bamboo which has tessellated leaf veins is hardy ; indeed we know that there are many Bamboos with tessellated venation which, from their habitat, cannot be grown in this country. Only one thing is certain, viz. that no Bamboo introduced up to the present has proved hardy that has not such tessellation.

It is a strange coincidence that Chamærops excelsa, the one Palm which is hardy in this country, has tessellated leaf veins. Latania borbonica, which is hardy in the South of France, has the leaf veins very slightly tessellated. I

have examined many of the tender Palms and found that
all have striated leaf veins. What can be this mysterious
connection between tessellation and hardiness ?

Mr. Thiselton Dyer, the director of Kew Gardens, to
whom I communicated this observation, writes to me:
"There must be something important behind a character
like this, and no doubt when we discover it, it will be a key
to other things."

The accompanying illustration, drawn by Mr. Brebner
of the microscopic laboratory at Kew, shows the difference
between tessellated and striated venation.

"The leaf *A* is of THAMNOCALAMUS FALCONERI, and *A'* shows
the fine venation between two of the coarser parallel veins
marked *v*.   The latter magnified 15 diameters, *i.e.* Fig. *A'*.

" The leaf *B* (nat. size) is of BAMBUSA DISTICHA (Mitford),
and its finer venation is shown at *B'* (× 15).

"The tessellated venation at *C'* is of ARUNDINARIA JAPONICA,
but the leaf itself was too big to figure."

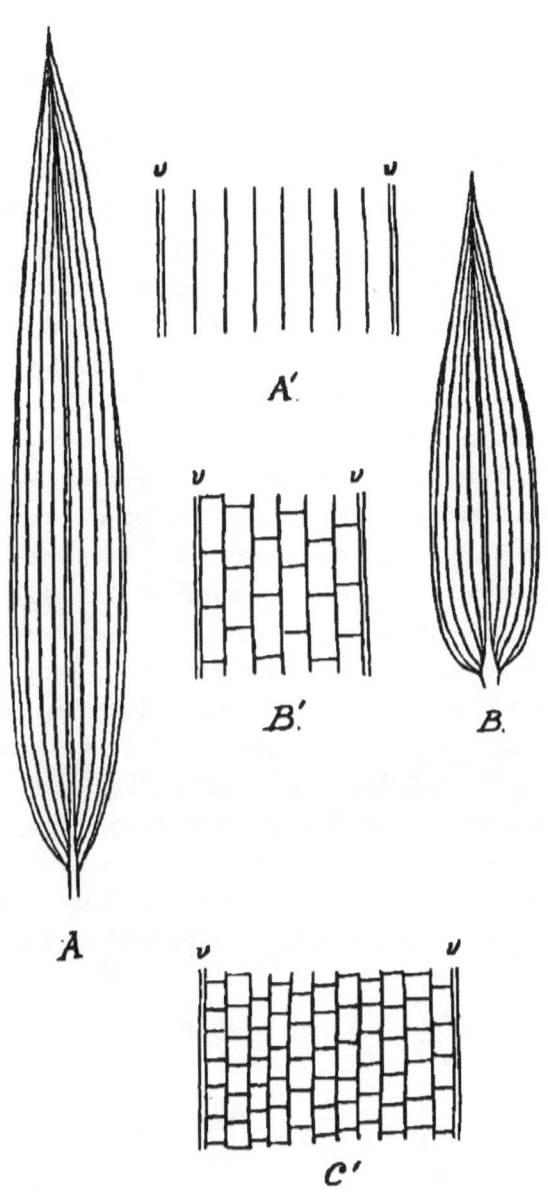

TESSELLATED AND STRIATED VENATION OF LEAVES OF BAMBOO

CHAPTER VI

ALLUSION has already been made to the uncertain state of
the nomenclature of the hardy Bamboos. Nor is this confusion to be wondered at. In the absence of flowers and
fruit science has not· declared herself, and the plants are
named and sent out by nursery gardeners according to their
own sweet fancy, and sometimes, though this may be an
ill-natured suspicion, according to the state of their stock.
. For instance, I have written to various nursery gardeners
' for Phyllostachys bambusoides, P. viridi-glaucescens, P. violescens, Arundinaria Fortunei, and another variety, I forget
now which ; in each case I received Arundinaria Simoni.
I have known Phyllostachys mitis sent out for P. Quilioi, and
have myself when asking for P. mitis been furnished with P.
Quilioi, aurea, and viridi-glaucescens, with a few plants of
the true P. mitis intermixed. Even at Kew Phyllostachys
bambusoides was for years represented by a ˙magnificent
plant of P. viridi-glaucescens. Indeed, Phyllostachys bambusoides presented itself to me in so many shapes, that I
began to look upon it as the Mrs. Harris of Bamboos, and
became as sceptical as to its existence as Betsy Prig. At
last, in 1894, the true plant was received at Kew from

Hong-Kong, and by the kindness of the director I have been furnished with a specimen of it.

The first serious attempt to clear up the fog surrounding this difficult subject has been made by Mr. Bean, the distinguished cultivator under whose care the collection of Bamboos at Kew has grown into a lovely garden, skilfully arranged with a view to exhibiting to their best advantage the grace and beauty of the plants. In a series of articles, which appeared in the *Gardeners' Chronicle* in the early part of the year 1894, Mr. Bean has very carefully and lucidly described the hardy Bamboos in cultivation at Kew. But even he, since those articles were written, has seen reason to modify some of the views which he then took as to the identity of certain species. The Kew plants have now been compared with those of other collections, and with the dried specimens in the herbarium, and the result of these investigations has been the revision of the nomenclature of the hardy Bamboos in accordance with the list given below, which, endorsed as it is by the high authority of Kew, may, it is hoped, be considered as final so far as the species at present in cultivation are concerned. Several of the species have, for the reasons given in each case, been renamed.

NATIVES OF CHINA AND JAPAN

ARUNDINARIA SIMONI

THIS, the tallest of our Arundinarias, and, with the exception of PHYLLOSTACHYS MITIS, of our hardy Bamboos, was introduced into France in 1862 by M. Simon, French Consul in China, and named after him by Carrière, who described the plant.[1] In the Bamboo Garden at Kew old-established specimens have reached the height of 18 feet with a circumference of 3 inches. My own plants in their fourth summer grew to 13 feet, and, in spite of the disastrous check of the month of February, the succeeding shoots last summer (1895) maintained the same height. In warmer climates the young shoots usually appear early in May. Here, unfortunately, they do, not begin to pierce the earth until midsummer, and, as they go on being produced until late in the autumn, the result is that a number of culms are born which cannot ripen and are surely doomed to die. These are apt to give the plant an untidy appearance and, being an eyesore, have to be removed. Like most of its genus, ARUNDINARIA SIMONI has a round stem, tapering off and slightly flattened at the apex, but less so than is the case in many of the Arundi-

[1] Curiously enough Munro's monograph of 15th November 1866 makes no mention of this species.

narias. Before the branches are developed it is furnished from top to bottom with sheaths, the upper edges of which are fringed. These sheaths vary in size according to their position on the stem. being very short at the bottom (though at this point they are longer than and overlap the internodes) and increasing in size towards the middle until they are 8 or 10 inches in length. Their colour is at first a fine green shading to purple, but soon fades to a dull yellow. At its top the sheath, as it were, divides itself longitudinally into two parts—the ligule and the limbus, or blade. (1) The ligule is a narrow elliptic membrane cut straight at the top like a scale, about one-sixteenth of an inch deep, which adheres closely to the stem and prevents the rain from running down between it and the sheath and so attacking the bud—the future branch of which the sheath is the natural guardian. On either side the limbus, curling slightly back, forms, as it were, two grooves which serve as channels to turn the water into its proper course. On the lower sheaths the ligule is, as a further protection, fringed with hairs, which are imperceptible on the upper sheaths. (2) The limbus, or blade, is a leaf-like appendage standing out at an angle from the sheath, or curving over, narrow and lanceolated, smooth on the upper surface, and slightly ribbed on the lower, with a fine serration on both edges. It is green at first, and often striped with white, but soon withers to a dull brownish straw colour. The limbus is very variable in length and breadth being from 3 to 4 inches long, and from a quarter to half an inch wide.

At first sight the blade has the appearance of a true leaf; but on examination it will be seen that it differs from a leaf in having no midrib, the nerves being numerous (sometimes

as many as twelve) and of equal size. At the very top of
the culm, however, the last four or five blades have a distinct
midrib and assume the character of true leaves. Both the
sheath and the blade are in a green state tessellated, but this
tessellation disappears when the parts wither. Under the
lens the sheath is seen to be covered with a thick silvery
white down, which acts as a waterproof coat protecting the
stomata. Between the sheath and the stem, as a further provision against the attacks of water, is secreted a thick coating
of white waxy bloom, which may be scraped off with the finger-
nail. It is found in the greatest profusion immediately
under the projecting nodes, and diminishes in quantity until
within about 1 inch or 1½ inch of the top of the node, below
which it almost disappears, being formed again under the
next rim. The lower part of the internode being entirely
encircled and guarded by the sheath does not stand in need
of this protection of the transpiratory organs against moisture ;[1]
but as the culm is drawn up, the sheath, narrowing away to
the ligule, leaves the upper part of each internode uncovered,
while in the meantime the waxy secretion has been formed
and so the bared portion of the stem has a sufficient protector.
When the sheath finally falls off, the whole of the internode
is found to be finely powdered with a delicate bloom.

The limbus, or blade, soon breaks away from the sheath
and disappears, but the ligule remains with the sheath, falling
and dying with it. The lower and upper joints of the culm
are far shorter than those in the middle, where they reach
their maximum.

When the culm has reached its full height branching

[1] *Vide supra*, p. 45.

begins to take place on the upper part, which takes precedence
of the lower. The manner of the branching is as follows.
If you strip off with a penknife the closely adherent sheath
of a culm approaching maturity, you will see a little, flat,
dome-shaped bud composed of a number of scales resting upon
a tiny cushion, formed by a very thin membrane in the axil
of the sheath, beautifully fringed with silken hairs to keep
out moisture, and fitting closely into a slight depression in
the stem. Take a more forward culm and the dome has
developed into a number of tiny spires with one tall steeple
in the middle, which grow and swell until they are meta-
morphosed into a bundle of branches from nine to thirteen
in number, some smaller, some bigger, but the longest, which
was the steeple, always in the middle. The sheaths are
forced away from the stem by the vigorous growth of the
purple branchlets, and the little silken cushion, which formed
the bed of the bud, having no longer any duty to perform
withers and is no more seen.

The branches are, of course, borne upon alternate sides of
the culm, which, as they are longer than the internodes and
rather upright, gives a false air of complete verticillation.

As with the internodes of the culm, so with those of the
branchlets, each internode is wrapped in its little sheath of a
purplish colour ending in a ligule and a blade, which is the true
leaf. But the ligule is, in proportion to the size of the sheath,
longer and rounder than those of the culm, and bears, moreover,
a conspicuous growth of little curly silky hairs. The tessellated
leaf varies much in size. An average measurement is about
10 inches long by three-quarters of an inch broad. It shows
a handsome green colour on the upper surface, more glaucous

below, serrated on both edges. Both surfaces are apparently smooth, but a lens reveals a thick white down, especially on the under side. The midrib, which is very prominent on the lower surface, is flanked on each side by about six secondary nerves, palpable to the touch. The leaf tapers off to a fine point at one end, and to a petiole about an eighth of an inch long at the other. Mr. Bean remarks (*Gardeners' Chronicle*, 10th March 1894): " It is curious that on the under surface of the leaf one side only of the midrib is glaucous, the other half green." This distinction is, so far as I can observe, only conspicuous towards the tip of the leaf where it begins to taper off. In a young state the leaves are often striped with a silver variegation.

It often happens that for some years, until it is thoroughly established, ARUNDINARIA SIMONI only throws up dwarfed and slender shoots bearing very narrow and starved foliage, a puzzle and disappointment to the planter, who begins to think that he has got hold of a different species. But it is only a question of time and patience ; in the end the true character of the plant is sure to assert itself.

A portion of rhizome cut from a plant which has been growing for three summers in its present place, shows the following characteristics :—

A fistulous, underground stem about half an inch in diameter, the pipe—the walls of which are lined sparsely with a sort of white pithy down—being three-sixteenths of an inch in diameter. The pipe is hermetically closed by the prominent nodes at intervals of from $1\frac{1}{2}$ inch to 3 inches in length. It is round, and lacks both the depression and the groove, caused by the close packing of the scaly stem bud, which are to be found in the rhizome of Phyllostachys. Indeed, the characteristics of the two genera are as jealously guarded in the underground as in the overground stem. As is the case with the culms, each internode is wrapped in a sheath, richly stained at first with purple, but dying away to a dirty straw colour, and terminating in a ligule and limbus or blade; but this latter appendage is not easy to find, as it is very quickly deciduous and is lost in the earth. These sheaths differ from the sheaths of the culm in their venation, which is not tessellated, and in the parallel veins being broader than those of the overground stem. In the axil formed by the base of its guardian sheath is the scaly stem-bud, appearing alternately on the knots on each side of the rhizome. These buds are not so flat as those of the culm, but are convex and bulge out. They are brilliantly enamelled, of a creamy white colour, and the outer scales being fringed, to guard against any danger from water, they look, in an early stage before the scales begin to separate, like shark's teeth. The nodes are encircled by verticillate roots without nodes or joints, each of which is covered with innumerable curly rootlets arranged in no symmetrical order. These roots pierce and tear their way through the sheaths which are thus, in the fulness of time, forced away from the parent rhizome and perish in the earth. The rhizome then wears a beautifully polished surface like ivory, of the colour to which the Japanese artists stain their carved Nétsukés; but immediately below the node this ivory yellow is delicately clouded with green, shading off to purple, and here the lens reveals a clothing of very minute silvery down (another careful provision of Nature for warding off water), which in a much less conspicuous degree is continued along the whole length of the apparently smooth internode.

It is worthy of notice that the stem buds are laid horizontally on the nodes, and do not begin to point upwards until they swell and develop into active growth. They then curve upwards from the stem, keeping their flatter side close to it until they pierce the soil and are born into the outer world.

The extreme point of the rhizome is very sharp and as hard as horn, admirably adapted for piercing the stiffest soil. It appears to be composed of innumerable sheaths wrapped closely round one another, but easily separated with a penknife. From these the succeeding nodes and internodes are developed in regular procession; unless, indeed, when, having terminated its underground career, the point takes an upward course, and is promoted to the honours of a terminal culm. These terminal canes are generally of less stature than those which spring from the rhizome nearer to the parent plant, but as soon as they have arrived at maturity a whorl of roots is thrown out from one or more of the barren knots (barren, I mean, of branches) at the base of the stem; they, in their turn, form rhizomes, and so the multiplication proceeds.

The rhizomes, radiating in almost straight lines to all points of the compass from the axis of the stems, soon do away with any semblance of formality in the groups, giving a wild and picturesquely natural appearance to the planting.

ARUNDINARIA SIMONI has flowered and fruited not unfrequently in English gardens; but there never has been, so far as I can learn, any general flowering in this country.

F

Here and there an isolated plant, or portion of a plant, has borne seed, but without any signs of exhaustion to itself, and without its neighbours showing any appearance of following its example. Two instances are recorded (there may have been many others) in the year 1895—the one in Surrey, which I myself saw, the other in Cornwall.

This being the case, it may be as well to give some description of the flower and fruit, which I abridge from Messrs. Rivière's account of the flowering which took place in the gardens of the Luxembourg at Paris in 1876.

Flowers, hermaphrodite.

Inflorescence, a simple spike borne at the end of a branchlet springing from the node of ramification. The spike composed of five, six, seven, or eight spikelets, with a single flower, placed distichously.

The spikelet bearing one flower consists of (1) one glume, or chaff-like inferior bract; (2) one glumella, or small superior bract; (3) two diminutive paleolæ, or still smaller bracts; (4) three pendant stamens; (5) a pistil with a sessile stigma, bifid, feathery, and of a whitish colour.

A little before the complete development of the flower, the anther of one of the three stamens is lodged in the glume, while the other two are coupled in the glumella. But as soon as fecundation is about to take place, the glume and glumella separate themselves, the stamens escape from their bondage, while the stigma opens out its divisions to receive the pollen. Immediately afterwards the stamens lean to the same side, while the glume and glumella close upon one another so as to protect the ovary during its growth. As for the stamens, whose filaments are thus caught between the two bracts, they remain hanging and in time perish.

The fruit is about a quarter of an inch long. It bears some resemblance to a grain of rye, but is arched and ellipsoid, that is to say, pointed at the top and obtuse at the base. A deep furrow runs along the whole length of the fruit, with smaller irregular transverse furrows. The colour is shining and yellowish.

I have before me a ripe seed of A. SIMONI which I gathered in Surrey. The only difference that I can detect between it and the above account is that it is less arched than Messrs. Rivière's description and drawing, and I fail to detect the small transverse furrows.

Tall and stately, perfectly hardy, and a vigorous grower, this Bamboo has narrowly missed being a plant of the first value. Beautiful it certainly is for many months of the year, but unfortunately, as I have already pointed out, in spring and in the very early summer it generally has a ragged and shabby appearance, owing to the injury done by the storms and frosts of winter to those culms which are born in the late autumn. It recovers, however, at midsummer, and increases in favour as the year wears on.

I have endeavoured to give a somewhat minute description of this Bamboo (1) because it is so universally grown in English gardens; (2) because it is a very typical Arundinaria, worthy of study, as helping to a right understanding of its Chinese and Japanese congeners; and (3) because its size makes it a comparatively easy matter to observe its habits.

ARUNDINARIA SIMONI, *var.* STRIATA

Rather less in stature than the type, from which it differs
mainly in having the foliage striped with a silver variegation.
This, however, is very variable and not to be depended upon.
The rhizomes are quite as rampant as those of the type, and
equal caution must therefore be observed in selecting a place
where it may run about without doing mischief. It is sometimes sent out by nursery gardeners under the erroneous
names of BAMBUSA PLICATA and BAMBUSA MAXIMOWICZII. It
flowered but did not seed in Mr. Smith-Barry's garden in
Fota Island, Co. Cork, in the year 1893. I very much
doubt whether it be right to separate STRIATA from the type.
The variegation is as often absent from the former as it is
present in the latter.

The Japanese name NARIHIRA-DAKÉ (BAMBUSA NARIHIRA,
Marliac) is a synonym of ARUNDINARIA SIMONI. It was so
named after Narihira, the hero of a romance of the eleventh
century called the *Isé Monogatari*, one of the classics of
Japan, written in prose, with poetry interspersed. The name
of the author is not known. BAMBUSA NARIHIRA is sent out
by certain nursery gardeners as a distinct species, but there
is no doubt as to its identity with ARUNDINARIA SIMONI, and
the distinction cannot be maintained.

ARUNDINARIA JAPONICA or MÉTAKÉ

A TALL and handsome plant, generally grown in gardens under the name of BAMBUSA MÉTAKÉ. The word MÉTAKÉ, or, more correctly, MÉDAKÉ, means in Japanese "female Bamboo," but there is no scientific reason for using the word "female" in connection with this species, any more than there is for calling the DENDROCALAMUS STRICTUS of India the "male" Bamboo.

The culms, which are round and green, grow to a height of 10 to 11 feet, with a circumference of half an inch to 2 inches. They are straight and slightly flattened at the top. When the branches of the second year make their appearance the stems are slightly arched by the weight of the foliage. The internodes are from 6 to 8 inches long, the pipe about an eighth of an inch in diameter. The sheaths, on which a roughness caused by minute bristles is distinctly perceptible, reach to about a distance of an inch from the next internode to that from which they spring, and on the upper part of the stem overlap it. They wither very early and are very persistent, so that the culm for the greater part of its length has the appearance of being completely encased by them. The ligule is about an eighth of an inch deep, slightly convex or flat on the upper edge, deeply concave on the lower. The limbus is very narrow, sometimes not more than an eighth of an inch broad, and from 1 to 2 inches long. The topmost sheaths terminate in a true leaf instead of a limbus. The sheath and limbus have the same irregular and evanescent appearance of tessellation noticed in the preceding species. A single branch is borne in the axil of the node and sheath, and hence the bud is a simple flattish scale, differing from the complex scaly bud of ARUNDINARIA SIMONI. The nodes are not very prominent. As the branches, which are two or three times as long as the internodes, are developed, the sheaths of the culms are forced back and roll themselves tightly round the lower part of the branches. There is very little of the waxy bloom so conspicuous on A. SIMONI to be found about the nodes and on the stem.

The leaves are from 8 to 12 inches long, by 1½ to 2 inches broad; the upper surface smooth and shining, the lower glaucous, felted with minute silvery hairs, and wrinkled longitudinally by the prominent secondary nerves, of which I have counted as many as nine on either side of the midrib. The edges, especially on one side, are very finely serrated.

The creeping rootstock in well-established plants travels far afield, so care must be taken to give this Bamboo plenty of room.

It has been the fashion rather to undervalue ARUNDINARIA JAPONICA, and as it is the most generally cultivated, so also it is the best abused, of all Bamboos. Messrs. Rivière say : " Ses gaines sèches, mais persistantes, lui donnent un aspect peu agréable . . . En somme il n'offre qu'un intérêt fort médiocre, et nous ne serions pas étonnés qu'il fût relégué tôt ou tard dans les jardins botaniques." Mr. Bean, in his description of the plant, cites a curious statement communicated by Signor Fenzi, an Italian horticulturist, to the *Gardeners' Chronicle* in 1872, to the effect that ARUNDINARIA JAPONICA is not a plant to be recommended for cultivation, being affected by a curious disease which causes its culms always to go into flower instead of growth, etc. This criticism is partly borne out by Messrs. Rivière, who assert that it has been in many instances observed in Algeria that this Bamboo, in certain cases, has a tendency to dwindle away instead of developing itself. If left to itself, say Messrs. Rivière, in an uncultivated spot, it ends by reaching the condition of an herbaceous plant, its spikelets, accompanied by two leaves, being carried upon little stems hardly ten centimetres high. In this degenerate condition, the inflorescence constitutes an ear or spike, long, slender, compact, bearing long and pendulous stamens. This is a state of things which I have never observed, and I am glad to see that Mr. Bean is, like myself, inclined to take up the cudgels for an old friend. He says : " There can be no doubt of its value to-day as a hardy evergreen." With that opinion I entirely agree. Given favourable conditions of soil and position, ARUNDINARIA JAPONICA grows, with time, into a striking and handsome object. I never saw it better shown than in a garden on the borders of Epping Forest, where, upon a promontory jutting out into a piece of ornamental water, and with a most picturesque background, it has quite a tropical appearance. The plant was first introduced in 1850 by Von Siebold, the eminent naturalist who did so much to make known the Flora and Fauna of Japan, in those days a closed country— except to the Dutch, whose factory on the island of Deshima, near Nagasaki, was the sole link of communication between the Land of the Rising Sun and the outer world. A Bavarian by birth, Von Siebold, some sixty years ago, attached himself as physician to the Dutch Mission, where, taking advantage of his rare opportunities, he laboured assiduously in every branch of natural history, to the great enrichment of the knowledge of the world.

As we have seen above (pp. 6, 7), ARUNDINARIA JAPONICA flowered and fruited in the Bois de Boulogne in Paris, and simultaneously all over France and in Algiers in the year 1867 or 1868.

Two years ago I received from Japan, through the Yokohama Gardeners' Association, several specimens of a Bamboo called in Japanese YA-DAKÉ, or the Arrow Bamboo. This they claimed to be PHYLLOSTACHYS BAMBUSOIDES, with which it has no more affinity than it has with a rosebush. The native name is due to the straight round culms being used for making arrows. It appears to be no more than a form of ARUNDINARIA JAPONICA; indeed, in its present young state, there is no difference to be detected. If anything, it appears to run more freely at the roots. Evidently, however, the Japanese gardeners consider YA-DAKÉ and MÉ-TAKÉ to be two different plants. It is quite possible that my plants were sent out as YA-DAKÉ by a mistake in the nursery, a mistake, however, which was repeated in those received from the same source at Kew.

ARUNDINARIA NITIDA

By far the daintiest and most attractive of all its genus,
ARUNDINARIA NITIDA possesses the additional advantage of
quite exceptional hardihood. Indeed it may be said to have
been the hero of the dire months of January and February
1895; for in the latter half of March, when the frost at last
yielded, while almost all the other Bamboos had their leaves
scorched to a dirty bay colour, this brave little plant was as
green and fresh and valiant as ever.

The story of this lovely species is somewhat curious.
When the Bamboo Garden was being formed at Kew, Mr.
Bean came across it in Messrs. Veitch's collection at Combe
Wood, where it was then named BAMBUSA NIGRA, from which
(a Phyllostachys), of course, it is absolutely distinct. At
that time the only Arundinaria known to have black stems
was the Himalayan A. KHASIANA, and with this species, which
had been somewhat perfunctorily described by Munro (though
indeed, in justice, it must be said that he called attention to
its striated venation and to its similarity to A. FALCATA),
the plant now under notice was conjecturally identified. As
ARUNDINARIA KHASIANA, accordingly, it was described by Mr.
Bean in the *Gardeners' Chronicle* and by myself in the
Garden. Attention, however, was called to the subject by

Mr. Gamble's monograph of the Bambuseæ of British India, from which it is clear that this Arundinaria agrees only in its purple-black stems with A. KHASIANA (which is closely allied to, and indeed hard to distinguish from, A. FALCATA), and, moreover, that there is not among the Bambuseæ of the Himalayas any known plant corresponding with it.

So it became necessary to find a fatherland and a history for this unknown waif. At the request of the Director of Kew, Messrs. Veitch made a careful search in their books and ascertained that their plant was raised from seed received in 1889 from Dr. Regel, then Director of the Botanic Garden of St. Petersburg. Professor Batalin, the present Director, on being written to, very kindly set the question at rest by informing the authorities at Kew that the seed was collected by the Russian traveller, Mr. Potanin, in North Szêchuan. He has since sent authentic specimens grown under glass in the St. Petersburg Botanic Garden from Mr. Potanin's seed, which leave no doubt as to their identity with the (misnamed) KHASIANA Hort. Kew.

The same plant has since been detected in the herbarium of Dr. Henry, who found it in Hu-pei.

As this ARUNDINARIA had not hitherto been described (except, as I have pointed out, under a false title) it was also necessary to give it a name, and I chose "NITIDA" as appropriate to its brilliancy and beauty (see Gardeners' Chronicle, xviii., 1895, p. 186).

An exceptional interest attaches to the discovery of the true home of ARUNDINARIA NITIDA as bearing out the belief of the Director of Kew that new additions to our collections of hardy Bamboos might be expected from the north-west of

China, into which region, as was first pointed out by Mr. H. I. Elwes, there is a marked extension of the Himalayan Flora.

We are as yet without any knowledge of the height to which ARUNDINARIA NITIDA will ultimately grow. When it was first received at Kew it was about a foot high; in its second year it grew to 6 feet 6 inches; and now in its third year it has grown to 8 feet 6 inches.

The culms are very slender, about a third of an inch in diameter, in their first year growing straight and rush-like, with somewhat prominent nodes about 3 inches, or rather more, apart. The sheaths are purple in colour, downy, with the ellipsoid ligule devoid of hairs; and the very narrow limbus or blade at the top of the sheath three-quarters of an inch in length, a bright green. The stem is surmounted by a tassel or plumelet of one, two, or three true leaves borne on the topmost sheaths. In the second year of the culm's life the branches, generally four in number, one of them being a little longer than the others, break away from the axils of the sheaths, which then wither and fall off. Each branch, as a rule, bears four leaves. Up to this time the culm remains quite upright; but in the third year innumerable branchlets, each in its turn bearing two or three leaves, are developed from the old branches, bearing down the stems in a perfect cascade of greenery all round the plant, and out of this fountain spring the culms of the previous year, overtopped again by the reedy stems of the new year, the whole forming a matchless picture of grace and elegance.

The leaves are from 2 to 3 inches long by about half an inch wide. Nothing can exceed the brilliancy of their green,

contrasting rarely with the deep black purple of the culms,
especially when a slight breeze reveals the rather glaucous
tinge of the under surface. In shape they are like a surgeon's
lancet rounded off to a somewhat blunted base, which ter-
minates in a petiole so short that the leaves have almost the
appearance of being sessile. What apology for a petiole exists
is tinged with purple, the colour being continued along the
edge of the leaf where it fades away into the point. One
edge is serrated, the other partially so. The secondary nerves,
three or four on either side, are very faint and inconspicuous, sometimes so hardly to be distinguished from the
longitudinal parallel lines of the tessellated venation as to
tempt one at first sight to think that they are absent.

In bulk, as in height, ARUNDINABIA NITIDA increases year
by year with great rapidity. It should therefore have plenty
of room to show off its full beauty. It is a modest and re-
tiring plant, dreading the full light of day. A touch of the
sun's rays suffices to curl up its leaves, which open out again
as soon as a passing cloud, or a friendly bough, gives it the
mantle of its protection. It must therefore be planted in the
shade of some choice woodland nook, whose beauty it will
adorn in winter as in summer.

According to Mr. Stapf, this species is nearest allied to
ARUNDINABIA SINICA, Hance (ARUNDINABIA LONGIBAMEA,
Munro). (*Kew Bulletin*, January 1896, p. 20.)

ARUNDINARIA VEITCHII

ARUNDINARIA (OR BAMBUSA?) VEITCHII

IN its general habit this Bamboo has many points of similarity with BAMBUSA PALMATA, though it is on a much humbler scale, the plant being only about 2 feet high and the leaves far smaller and more suddenly pointed at the top. The culms are round and much flattened at their summits, but their colour, unlike those of BAMBUSA PALMATA, is a rich purple. The nodes are not very salient, the internodes being from 3 to 4 inches long. The circumference of the culms is about half an inch or a little more, the pipe about one-sixteenth of an inch in diameter. Each node bears only one branch. The leaf sheaths, which show no tessellation, have a very small ligule and limbus with serrated edges, and on either side of the ligule is a little tuft of coarse hairs, sometimes standing out like a stag's antlers. These hairs, together with the limbus, are very perishable and soon lost, while the sheaths are very persistent, encircling the culm until the branches stand out. The purple internodes are plentifully bedecked with bloom.

The tessellated leaves are about 7 inches long by some 2¼ inches broad, green on the upper surface, glaucous underneath, and much serrated. Rounded at the base, towards the upper end they are pinched in, rather more on one side than on the other, and culminate in a short, sharp point. They are markedly serrated on both edges. The yellowish midrib is very prominent, and has about eight secondary nerves on either side of it. The glaucous colour on the under side is, as usual, caused by a thick felting of very minute silvery down. The petiole is purple on the upper side, yellow on the lower. The edges of the leaves wither in late autumn, giving the plant, during the winter, a variegated, but somewhat shabby appearance; but the thick new foliage which comes with the renewal of spring is very beautiful, and for covering what Professor Sargent calls "the forest-floor," and ousting all weeds and noxious rubbish, this little Bamboo is invaluable. Once it is established nothing can stop it. The Japanese call it KUMA-ZASA,[1] "the edged dwarf Bamboo"; but unfortunately Munro, in his ignorance of the language, has given that name to another species. (See the remarks below on PHYLLOSTACHYS KUMASASA or VIMINALIS.) I am told on good authority that some botanists claim this species as belonging to the Bambusæ veræ, or true Bamboos.

BAMBUSA SENANENSIS

A plant was received last year from Japan under this name. I cannot at present detect any difference between it and ARUNDINARIA VEITCHII. However, Mr. Watson, of Kew, tells me that some botanists regard it as a distinct species. The Japanese name for it is YAKIBAZASA, the "sword-edged dwarf Bamboo." There is another Bamboo, a tall species used for making furniture, etc., which also goes by the name of SENANENSIS, and which the Japanese call SUDZU-DAKÉ, the "Reed Bamboo."

[1] Or Kokumazasa, "the lesser-edged Bamboo," when the name Kumazasa is applied to Bambusa palmata.

BAMBUSA PALMATA

A STRIKINGLY beautiful and most effective species, conspicuous from the great size of its leaves, which are often used by Japanese peasants to wrap up the bit of salt fish or other condiment which they eat with their rice.

The culms with me are about 5 feet high, and about an inch in circumference. Their colour is bright green powdered with waxy bloom, especially below the internodes. The main part of the stem is round, but it is much flattened at the top. The nodes are not very prominent; and the sheaths, which early in life fade to straw colour, are very persistent half-way up the internode, which is from 5 to 6 inches long, varying little in length over the greater part of the stem. The fistulous character of the stem is inconspicuous at its base, but towards the middle of the culm the pipe is about an eighth of an inch in diameter. The hairless sheaths, which adhere closely to the stem, are surmounted by a small equally hairless ligule and a limbus or blade, which is often very minute and always shortlived. I can detect no true cross veins in the sheaths, which with their broad parallel veins, dotted with pellucid glands, greatly resemble the underground sheaths of ARUNDINARIA SIMONI. The limbus, however, is quite conspicuously tessellated. The ligule is fringed, but so

minutely as to deceive the naked eye. The limbus is
serrated on both edges. The branches being single, it follows
that the bud-scale at the axil of the sheath differs from that
of ARUNDINARIA SIMONI in being simple; it is also narrower
than the complex bud of the latter species. The internodes
of the single branch are about as long as those on the
culm.

The leaves constitute the chief beauty of the plant. They
are from 12 to 13 inches long by 3 to 3½ inches broad,
pinched in about an inch from the end and tapering rather
suddenly to a very fine point. Both edges are serrated with
very sharp teeth. The base of the leaf is rounded off and
ends in a stout petiole. The midrib is very prominent and
conspicuous, being of a yellowish colour and glabrous. It is
flanked on either side by a dozen or thirteen beautifully-
defined secondary nerves, and the network of the tessellation
is close and very conspicuous. The colour of the leaves is a
brilliant green above, smooth and shining, while the under
surface is of a glaucous colour, covered with a very minute
down visible with a lens, the secondary nerves carrying, here
and there, tiny white hairs more prominent than the rest, but
still invisible without a magnifying glass.

The rhizome is strong, sharply pointed, and very active,
travelling far. This Bamboo seems to thrive equally well
under full sunshine or in deep shade; but it always appears
to me that the creeping rhizome is inclined to travel more
in the direction of shade, as if it were seeking its natural
home.

A bold group of BAMBUSA PALMATA with a background of
Hollies, and associated with Lady Ferns and such sympathetic

compatriots as Funkia Sieboldii, Anemone japonica (which always seems to show to its best advantage under shade), and Ophiopogon, is a very striking and ornamental object, which even the most careless observer never passes by unnoticed.

The Japanese evidently consider BAMBUSA PALMATA and ARUNDINARIA VEITCHII (see p. 77) to be intimately related, for many of their gardeners give the name KUMAZASA to both, only distinguishing the latter species as the "lesser KUMAZASA."

BAMBUSA TESSELLATA or RAGAMOWSKI

THIS striking Bamboo belongs to the same type, as regards form, as BAMBUSA PALMATA and BAMBUSA VEITCHII It is a very beautiful species, noteworthy as having the largest leaves of any of our hardy Bamboos.

Munro described and named it, giving the genus as doubtful. Indeed his opportunities were limited, for as he himself says, "I have only seen the dried leaves of this species when sewn together and in the state so largely used by the Chinese in packing their tea."

The stem is about 2½ feet high, round, and a little over half an inch in girth; the pipe exceedingly small, sometimes quite minute, hardly more than would admit a horse's hair. At the top the stem is flattened. The nodes are so little prominent as to be hardly palpable to the touch; indeed so remarkable is this, that at first sight one might be tempted to think that the long sheaths, which closely and persistently enwrap the stem, all spring from one node. If these are taken off with a penknife, the nodes appear at short distances of from 1 to 2 inches, each bearing a long sheath encircling not only the stem but the lower parts of two or three sheaths immediately above it, so that the culm has the appearance of being thicker at the top than at the bottom, whereas the reverse is the case.

The persistent sheaths, which soon wither to a dull straw colour, have a few rare cross veins and are therefore partially tessellated, being fringed on the lower part of their edges with very soft brown hairs, and are downy where they are covered by the successive wraps of the lower sheaths. The ligule and the limbus vary much in size. The former is arched at the top, and furnished at the sides with two or three coarse hairs ; the latter is very narrow, sometimes quite short, sometimes over 2 inches in length. Like the sheath, it is imperfectly and capriciously tessellated.

It will be seen by the above description that every device is adopted by Nature to ward off the arch-enemy, damp.

The node gives birth to one solitary branch. I once only found twins springing from one and the same node.

The leaves are 18 inches and more long by rather over 4 inches wide, tapering beautifully to a fine point. The upper surface is a bright and shining green, the under surface glaucous. The midrib, on one side of which Munro notices a tomentose line, is broad and prominent, a yellowish white in colour, and on either side are sometimes as many as from fifteen to eighteen secondary nerves from one-eighth to one-sixteenth of an inch apart. At the base the midrib ends in a strong petiole slightly stained with purple. The edges of the leaves are sharply serrated. Munro describes the leaf from his dried specimen as glabrous, but, in the living plant, the lens shows a minute covering of silvery hairs, especially on the lower surface to which they give its glaucous colour.

In the mature plant the foliage arches over, borne down

by its own weight, and forming a carpet through which the young culms spring up with pretty effect.

When once established, the rhizome is very active and sends up new shoots at some distance from the parent plant.

BAMBUSA ANGUSTIFOLIA

I HAVE renamed this dainty species, which, so far as I can ascertain, has not hitherto been described, on account of the obvious convenience of giving it a title by which it may be recognised. The French nursery gardeners send it out as BAMBUSA VILMORINI.

It is a lovely little Bamboo, perhaps an ARUNDINARIA, with very slender, round culms, about a foot in height and about a quarter of an inch or less in circumference. The piping is exceedingly minute. The nodes, which are rather prominent for such a Lilliputian, are from 1 inch to 1¼ inch apart. The colour of the stem is light green shading to purple. The branches are borne singly or in pairs, but as they are much longer than the internodes the plant has at first sight an appearance of being many-branched. The sheaths, which are not very persistent, are slightly downy, and the almost imperceptible ligule is armed with a few very fine long white hairs. The limbus is very small, as befits the rest of the members. The leaves which are from 2 to 4½ inches in length by from three-sixteenths to a quarter of an inch in width, at once suggest the name ANGUSTIFOLIA. They are tessellated, serrated on both edges, and sometimes striped with white. They taper to a fine point, being pinched in about half an

inch from the end. The lower end is somewhat abruptly
rounded off to a comparatively stout little petiole. There
are generally three secondary nerves on either side of the
midrib, but sometimes only two.

Small as this Bamboo is its prettiness is so charming that
it is worthy of a choice position in any collection. It runs
apparently pretty freely at the roots, but is not likely to make
such a good carpet as its even smaller relation BAMBUSA
PYGMÆA.

BAMBUSA NAGASHIMA

THIS is apparently another dwarf Bamboo, with me very
small, at present in its third year, but as it has been checked
by transplanting, it may possibly, with time, increase in
stature, still it must always be on a very small scale indeed.

The culms, which are round and slender and of a purplish
green colour, are about a foot or 18 inches high, and hardly a
quarter of an inch in circumference. They are flattened at
the top. The pipe is very diminutive. The internodes are
about an inch and a half in length. The nodes are well defined,
and have a shining purple band round their base, with a
protection of waxy bloom beneath them. The sheaths on
the middle and upper parts of the stem overlap the succeeding node, leaving, however, a portion of their own particular
internodes bare. The ligule and limbus are very minute, the
former bearing a tuft of delicate white hairs on either side, a
feature which is more conspicuous towards the top of the
culm. The leaves are sometimes as much as 5½ inches long
by three-quarters of an inch broad. They are tessellated,
serrated on both edges, and bright green in colour. They are
pinched in towards the top terminating in a fine point,
round at the base, and having a well-defined petiole. The
secondary nerves on each side of the midrib are from three to

four in number.   The main branches are borne singly, but the branchlets are in twos and threes.

I was at first rather inclined to undervalue BAMBUSA NAGASHIMA, but it certainly improves upon acquaintance ; and, having a distinction of its own, should certainly have a place in the Bamboo garden.   It has not hitherto shown any inclination to run, but as almost all the dwarf Bamboos have such very rampant rhizomes, I should not be surprised to see it throw up shoots at some distance from the main plant.

BAMBUSA QUADRANGULARIS

THIS curious and somewhat rare Bamboo, rare at any rate in cultivation in Europe, owes its name to its culms, which are square like the stems of some of the Labiatæ. This feature, however, though always in a greater or less degree present, is conspicuous only when the plant has attained some size. This it has not yet done, so far as I am aware, in outdoor cultivation in this country. Whether it will ever reach any height with us, except perhaps in some especially mild corner of our island, is an open question. The last two exceptional winters killed my plants down to the ground; but in spite of this the roots have shown extraordinary activity, throwing up shoots in every direction, each year stronger than the last. I have good hopes therefore that the plant may in time become acclimatised, the more so as the plants which suffered so severely were travel-sick the first year (1893), and so manifestly unfit to cope with a succession of adversities. They now, in the late summer of 1895, are growing with a vigour which is quite surprising when we consider what they have gone through. But even should they continue to die down every winter, I should still think them well worth growing for the beauty of their summer foliage. There is a good specimen in the temperate house at Kew.

In its native country this is a tall and stately Bamboo; groves of it, 30 feet high, are to be seen near Osaka, the Venice of Japan. In a culm about 12 feet high the nodes are about 4 to 5 inches apart, the stem is about seven-eighths of an inch in diameter, and the pipe nearly a quarter of an inch across. The nodes, which are square and, like the culm, rounded at the corners, are very prominent, and have a deep purple band on the lower side. The rest of the culm is a dark green shading to purple. The branches are from six to seven in number. On a dried culm round three sides of the square are seen little pits as if branches had been borne on all three sides, there are the traces left on two sides by rudimentary branches in the shape of little spines. The attachment of the branches is very peculiar, for when the stem is dry, or nearly so, they break off almost with a touch, leaving a little raised scar sometimes depressed in the centre. The texture of the sheath, which is shaded with purple and loosely tessellated, is very thin and delicate, and it is much more open than in most Bamboos, gaping from the base and leaving the greater part of the internode uncovered. The upper sheaths overlap the succeeding node. The ligule and limbus are exceedingly diminutive, the former being very imperceptibly fringed with delicate hairs. The shape of the bud in the axil of the sheath is very peculiar; it is something like a flattened Hyacinth bulb in miniature, and is stained with red. The leaves are of a fine deep green, about 8 inches long by 1 inch in width, serrated on both edges. The tessellation is very minute and beautifully close. A fair-sized leaf shows seven secondary nerves on each side of the midrib. The shape is lanceolated, pinched in about an inch from the fine point, and tapering to a short petiole.

I have already alluded to the travelling power of the creeping rootstock.

It was supposed at one time that the square shape of the culms was due to their having been subjected to some artificial process of cramping, like the feet of Chinese ladies; but the young stems, even in their present very imperfect development, have sufficient character to disprove this.

It would be a great pity if this very interesting member of the Bamboo family, as ornamental as it is peculiar, should lack the vigour necessary to enable it to thrive with us. If any one should be tempted to import plants I should urge in their case, more even than in that of some of the other Bamboos, the importance of giving them the benefit of a winter indoors. In plant life much depends upon a good start; and I cannot help thinking that if I had taken this precaution, instead of planting my specimens out as soon as they were received in the month of November, they would have told a very different tale.

BAMBUSA LAYDEKERI

A SEMI-DWARF Bamboo, not, perhaps, one of the most attractive
of the family, but certainly peculiar enough to deserve a place ·
in a collection.

The culms are about 3 feet high, but the plant gives
promise of growing perhaps to twice that height. They are
round, green in colour, and stained with purple, about half
an inch in circumference. The piping is very small. The
nodes, which are prominent, are about 3 to 4 inches apart.
The branches, which on the lower nodes are borne singly, in
pairs, or in threes, are almost verticillate on the upper ones,
and, being long in proportion to the size of the plant, give it
a very characteristic appearance. The sheaths have a very
small ligule, fringed with delicate hairs which fall off quickly,
and an equally small limbus. The largest leaves are about
6 inches long by three-eighths of an inch in breadth; they taper
to a very fine point at the top, and have a well-defined petiole
at the base. The colour is a dark green, with a rather shabby
and unsatisfactory mottled variegation of a paler colour. The
secondary nerves are from three to five on either side of the
midrib. The leaves are tessellated, and more serrated on one
edge than on the other. The rhizome is very rampant.

Not a plant to be recommended for those who desire to
confine themselves to cultivating a few species.

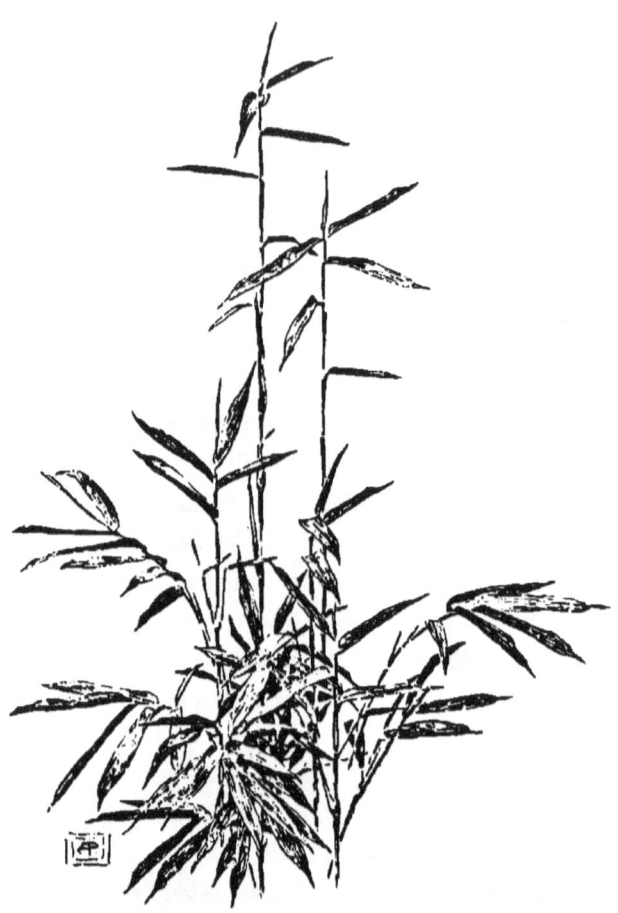

BAMBUSA LAYDEKERI

BAMBUSA MARMOREA

BAMBUSA MARMOREA

THIS Bamboo is sent out by Mr. Marliac under the name of BAMBUSA KAN-CHIKU. I have ventured to rename it, as it has not, so far as I know, been described, and the name KAN-CHIKU is somewhat confusing, as there is already a Bamboo called KANZAN-CHIKU, a synonym of ARUNDINARIA HINDSII. I have chosen the name MARMOREA on account of the very peculiar appearance of the young culms, which are folded in purple sheaths delicately marbled with a pinkish silver-gray, through which, near the knots, peep glimmers of the bright emerald green and dark purple of the stem itself. The plant is a semi-dwarf, not at present more than 3 feet high with me, but promising to grow taller in course of time. The purple stems, shading off to brilliant, are round and slender, about half an inch in circumference in the thickest part. It is solid throughout; the fistula, which is such a conspicuous feature in the structure of most Bamboos, being absent. The nodes are very prominent, especially on the side which carries the branches, where they project downwards. In colour, too, they are peculiar, for whereas in most of our Bamboos the purple colour of the stems is most noticeable about the nodes, in this the under side of the knot is bright green, however purple the rest of the internode may be. The

internodes are very short, not more than 1¼ inch, or at most
2 inches in length, in a culm 3 feet long. The marbled
sheaths, which are very loosely and irregularly tessellated,
are very thin, and have an almost imperceptible flat ligule
(which towards the top of the culm has a number of fine silky
hairs) and a very minute limbus. The sheaths have, moreover, a little very delicate felting at their junction with
the node. The branches are borne in threes, two short and
one long, and are very long in proportion to the internodes,
being in such a culm as I am describing as much as from
7 to 8 inches in length. The leaves are bright green, about
4¼ inches long by three-eighths to five-eighths of an inch
broad. They are serrated on both edges, prettily tessellated,
and are pinched in at about half an inch from the very sharp
point in so marked a manner that they seem to terminate in
a little tongue. The secondary nerves on either side of the
midrib are four or five in number. The petiole is short, the
rounded base of the leaves being almost sessile. The rhizome
is very active, new shoots appearing at a foot or more from
the main plant.

The length of the branches, which overlap each other and
are very upright, gives the dense foliage the appearance of
being verticillate, and the fully-developed culm assumes the
shape of a fox's brush.

As to the complete hardihood of BAMBUSA MARMOREA it
is a little difficult to pronounce a verdict. We have hardly
sufficient experience to judge. It passed unscathed through
the winter of 1893-94, braving 24° of frost. But the winter of
1895 killed it down to the ground. It must be said though
that the season was exceptional in many particulars. The

summer was wet and sunless, so the culms were not well
ripened ; the plants, moreover, were not thoroughly established
and were altogether at a considerable disadvantage.   In spite
of all this with the succeeding spring they shot up with great
vigour.   For two winters my plants have had absolutely no
protection.   If they had been screened with a little bracken
I think their case would have been different.   It is certainly
a very unique species, as pretty as it is strange, well worthy
of any pains that may be bestowed upon it.

ARUNDINARIA CHRYSANTHA

A SEMI-DWARF, capriciously variegated Bamboo, by some experts thought to be a variegated form of ARUNDINARIA HUMILIS, though it is an altogether taller plant. It differs materially from the golden ARUNDINARIA AURICOMA (p. 100), inasmuch as the lower surface of the leaf is markedly ribbed, and lacks the soft velvety down of the later species. On the other hand, the down on the sheaths is very conspicuous ; moreover, it is far less brilliant in colour, and the variegation is occasionally rather muddy and uncertain, a great portion of the plant retaining a uniform green colour, the brightness of which is clouded and dimmed by the tendency to variegation. Like ARUNDINARIA HUMILIS, ARUNDINARIA CHRYSANTHA runs freely at the roots, which ARUNDINARIA AURICOMA does not appear likely to do.

The highest culms which I have seen are from 4½ to 5½ feet high, but it will probably exceed that growth in time. The stem is fistulous, very slender, and round. The nodes are not prominent, but have rather a sharp lower rim, and the internodes are rarely more than an inch in length. The branches are numerous, giving an appearance of verticillation to the stems. The sheaths are very hairy on one edge. The ligule is conspicuous and fringed with delicate hairs. The limbus is very small and quickly falls off. The tessellated leaves are from 5 to 7 inches long by about half an inch or three-quarters broad. There are from four to six secondary nerves on each side of the midrib.

I am inclined to think better of this Bamboo as an ornamental plant than I was when I first made its acquaintance; still it is no great favourite of mine even now. Being neither frankly green nor frankly variegated, it is rather a disappointing plant. It has the merit of being perfectly hardy.

ARUNDINARIA PUMILA

A VERY pretty and ornamental little dwarf Bamboo. At first one might be tempted to confound this species with ARUNDINARIA HUMILIS, but closer observation leads to the conviction that it is quite a distinct plant. It is less tall, the leaves are a darker green, shorter, and not so broad, and do not taper so gradually to a point as those of ARUNDINARIA HUMILIS. The tessellation is closer, the teeth of the serrated edges are, if anything, less conspicuous, and the nodes are less well defined and far less downy; but, on the other hand, they have a waxy bloom not to be found in A. HUMILIS. The stem is much more slender and more entirely purple, except quite at the base.

The culms are about 15 inches high or rather more, round, and fistulous, very slender, about three-eighths of an inch in circumference, slightly flattened at the top. The nodes are not prominent, but well defined, with a deposit of waxy bloom on the under side. The internode is about 2½ inches long. The upper sheaths are very hairy at their base, but this feature is not present in those at the lower end of the culm. The ligule and limbus are small, the former without hairs, except towards the top of the stem where the sheath ends in a true leaf. The culms are not much branched.

The leaves are about 5 inches long by a half to three-quarters of an inch in breadth, rounded at the base, petiolated, and ending rather suddenly in a fine point. They are tessellated, serrated on both edges, and rather rough to the touch on both surfaces. Bright green in colour, a fully-developed leaf will have five secondary nerves on each side of the midrib.

Altogether a brilliant little plant, quite hardy, and a very effective ornament for some rocky nook, where, as it does not seem very much inclined to run at the roots, it may better be kept within bounds than some of its family.

ARUNDINARIA AURICOMA

A DWARF Bamboo, with exceedingly brilliant golden variegation, very ornamental, and worthy of a conspicuous position.

The culms are about 3 feet in height, round and slight in
structure, being only about a quarter of an inch in circumference. They are fistulous, but the piping is very diminutive.
The colour of the stems is purple. The nodes, which are not
prominent, are from 3 to more than 5 inches apart. The
lower rim of the node is dark and shining. The sheaths
are hairy at the base, and have the edges fringed with
delicate hairs (hardly visible except under a lens), more on
one side than on the other; they show very rare cross veins,
are tipped with a very narrow ligule and a tiny limbus which
is soon lost. On either side of the ligule is a tuft of two or
three curly hairs. The branches, which are long in proportion
to the height of the culm, are borne singly, or more rarely in
pairs. The leaves, which are boldly striped with bright yellow,
are from 5 to 7 inches in length by 1 inch in breadth; they
are pinched in at about half an inch from the sharp point,
more conspicuously on one side than on the other. The base
is rounded, and ends in a well-defined petiole. Both edges
are serrated, but the teeth are sharper on one side. A marked
character of the leaf is the velvety softness of the under

surface caused by the close felting of minute hairs with which it is covered. The upper surface is almost rough to the touch. The midrib is rather prominent, and is flanked on either side by about five secondary nerves. The tessellation is well defined.

Altogether a very striking plant. It is not apparently a very rampant runner.

It used to be called ARUNDINARIA or BAMBUSA FORTUNEI AUREA; but, as it has evidently no relationship with ARUNDINARIA FORTUNEI, I have renamed it.

ARUNDINARIA MAXIMOWICZII

Probably a synonym of the last species. I can detect no difference between them. The name MAXIMOWICZII is sometimes wrongly given to ARUNDINARIA SIMONI STRIATA, and I have also known BAMBUSA TESSELLATA, or RAGAMOWSKI, to be sent out by nurserymen under this title.

ARUNDINARIA FORTUNEI

A SILVER variegated dwarf Bamboo about 3 feet high. The stem is round, fistulous, green, and erect, but rather more zigzagged than some of the species of similar habit. The nodes, which are not very prominent, are often hidden by the overlapping sheaths. The internodes are seldom more than an inch apart. The sheath is rather thick for so small a Bamboo, fringed on one side with hairs visible under a lens, terminating in a narrow, strap-shaped ligule bearing tufts of hairs, and a very small limbus. The branches are long and borne singly or in pairs. The leaves are about 5 inches long by a half or three-quarters of an inch wide. They are tessellated, and both edges are serrated. They are pinched in towards the point, rounded at the base, and have a short white petiole. There are four or five secondary nerves on each side of the midrib. The colour is a bright green, with a pure white and beautifully conspicuous striped variegation. The plant loses its leaves in winter, but quickly recovers its beauty in the spring. The rhizome is active, and the plant should therefore be given room to run about at will.

A very pretty species.

ARUNDINARIA HUMILIS

COMMONLY called ARUNDINARIA FORTUNEI VIRIDIS, as if it were a green form of the silver variegated ARUNDINARIA FORTUNEI from which it is quite distinct in many essential particulars.

The culms grow to a height of from 2 to 3 feet. They are slender, fistulous, round, and slightly flattened at the top; and, though they are slightly zigzagged, the habit of the plant is erect. The internodes are from 2 to nearly 5 inches long. The nodes are not very prominent. The ramification is in twos and threes, and the branches are inordinately long in proportion to the length of the culm. On a stem of 30 inches I find two branches over 20 inches in length. The sheaths are of a purplish colour at first, withering to a dull straw colour. When young they are very hairy at the base, and perserve to the end a fringe of delicate hairs, visible under the lens, on one edge. The ligule is very small, slightly arched, and furnished with very minute hairs. The limbus is minute and soon drops off. The leaves, which are of rather a paler green than most Bamboos, show little difference in colour between the upper and lower surfaces. They are smooth, and serrated on both edges; about 4 to 6 inches in length, tapering to a very fine

point, the largest about seven-eighths of an inch in breadth.
The base is rounded and ends in a petiole. There are four
or five secondary nerves on each side of the midrib.

ARUNDINARIA HUMILIS is a very pretty plant, but with
me dies down in a hard winter. The following spring,
however, it shoots up with renewed vigour, and as the
rhizome is very active, it soon spreads over a large surface.

BAMBUSA FASTUOSA

HOWEVER difficult it may be to distinguish between some of the species of hardy Bamboos, this very stately and noble plant stands out quite conspicuously among its fellows. Tall, graceful, majestic, nobly plumed with a foliage which, for richness and colour, is without a rival, how can it fail to make a striking feature in the wild garden? It was first imported from Japan four years ago by M. Latour-Marliac of Temple-sur-Lot, and was, for the first time, sent out by him last year. Unfortunately, it is still very difficult to obtain. It was first described by me in the *Garden* newspaper at the beginning of 1895.

The culms of my plants are from 12 to 15 feet high, and rather more than 3 inches in circumference. In their first year they have thrown up new shoots nearly as important as the parent stems. The young culms are of a bright green colour, heavily splashed with purple-brown blotches. They are straight and very hollow, the wood being a mere shell and easily split. The internodes, which are grooved, are short, only from 5 to 6 inches long in a stem 15 feet high. The lower end of the culm for 2 or 3 feet is bare of branches. At first these appear in twos and threes, but higher up on the stem they become more numerous. I have counted

as many as seven or eight distinct branches of different
lengths on one node, and these again are much ramified,
the branchlets having several very short internodes. The
branches being much longer than the internodes and very
erect, the top of the culm appears in the distance to be
verticillated, like some of the Arundinarias, from which,
however, it differs in many points—notably in the grooved
internodes, and in the deciduous character of the sheaths.
These sheaths constitute one of the rare beauties of the
plant.   They are rather thick and felted on the outside,
shaded with a beautiful purple colour until they are pushed
aside by the young branches, wither, and fall off.   But even
in their death they are lovely, for the inner surface is stained
a deep claret colour, with a glaze which would do honour to
the finest specimens of Oriental pottery.   The ligule is small
and rather flat, fringed with delicate and very tiny silk hairs.
The limbus is long and narrow.   In a sheath before me it is
$3\frac{1}{2}$ inches in length by one-eight of an inch wide.   In a green
state both sheath and limbus are tessellated, but the cross
veins are not to be detected after withering has taken place.
The leaves are from 5 to 7 inches long by three-quarters of
an inch to 1 inch in breadth, tapering to a sharp point, and
markedly constricted at about an inch from the tongue-like
end.   The base of the leaf narrows rather gradually into a
long and well-defined petiole.   The veins are very closely
tessellated and both edges serrated, but, as is the case with so
many Bamboos, the teeth of the saw are far more prominent
on one side than on the other.   Both surfaces are smooth,
though there is a microscopic felting, especially on the under
face, which is roughly ribbed by the five or six secondary

nerves on either side of the midrib. The colour of the leaves is a brilliant green on the upper face, contrasted finely with a beautiful glaucous tint, which the least puff of air reveals on the lower. The rhizome, which shows sure signs of great activity—even the first year's shoots being well away from the old culm—is more fistulous than that of any Bamboo which I have observed. A section which I measured had an oval pipe in the internode of the rootstock a quarter of an inch long by one-eighth of an inch across.

BAMBUSA FASTUOSA is altogether a grand member of a beautiful family, and does justice to the somewhat pompous name with which M. Latour-Marliac has dignified it. He assures me, moreover, that it is one of the hardiest and most trustworthy of all the Bamboos. Of this I am unable to speak from personal experience, for the first specimens received in England were only planted out last spring, and they have not yet faced a hard winter in this country; but the unusual vigour with which they have grown, and their whole appearance are, so far, entirely in accord with the character which M. Marliac gives to the species.

ARUNDINARIA HINDSII

A VERY distinct and beautiful species sent out by French nurserymen as BAMBUSA ERECTA. The Japanese name is KANZAN-CHIKU. I have seen it described in French catalogues as *une espèce de serre*, and certainly it was cut down to the ground by the exceptional frost of February 1895; but as during the summer of the same year it grew again more vigorously than ever, both with me and at Kew, in an even more unpropitious climate, I have every hope of ac-climatising it. But, even should it have to be reduced to the rank of a perennial herb, it is well worth growing on account of its many distinctions and its ornamental habit. Munro only saw a fragment of a culm 18 inches high, and his description is therefore necessarily very imperfect, and indeed inaccurate.

The tallest culm which I have seen is about 7 feet high. The stem is round and very straight, hence the name "erecta." The rather long nodes are flat below, and prominent above, at the points where the fasciculated branches spring. The internodes are from 3 to 7 inches in length, smooth, and covered with a beautiful white waxy secretion like the bloom on a grape, making a fine contrast with the deep blue-green of the whole plant. The branches are quasi-verticillate and erect. The leaves, too, stand upright at first, but as they grow longer bend over with their own weight. They vary in length, some being as much as 9 inches long by about five-eighths of an inch broad. Their colour a dark glaucous green, of rather a lighter shade on the under side. They taper off to a longish petiole at the base, and are pinched in somewhat about an inch from the very fine point. They are thicker than is the case in most Bamboos, slightly hairy and serrate, especially on one edge. The veins are more conspicuously and beautifully tessellated than in any Bamboo that I have observed. The prominent secondary nerves are in number from four to six on each side of the midrib. The leaf sheaths, which are very persistent, are slightly hairy on the top.

This description applies to the plant in a young state. I have no doubt that with age its stature must increase greatly, and, at the same time, probably the size of the leaves and the length of the internodes of the stems.

This Bamboo has every appearance of running freely at the roots. Hong-Kong is given as the habitat of the species ; but Mr. Bean says that it is not included in the Flora of that island (*Gardeners' Chronicle*, 24th February 1894). It was, however, there that Hinds first found it in 1841. It is cultivated in Japan, but I have no knowledge as to whether it is indigenous there.

ARUNDINARIA HINDSII, *VAR.* GRAMINEA

A SMALLER plant altogether than the last species, but considered by the authorities at Kew to be another form of the same species. The culms of the plants which I have seen are rather over 4 feet high, very slender and delicate as compared with the type (No. 13), while the colouring is totally different. The dark glaucous pigment, looking as if indigo were one of its ingredients, is missing in the smaller species, the leaves of which are bright green, while the round, slender stem, so richly coloured in the type, is yellowish, and lacks, moreover, the waxy bloom to which I have alluded. The internodes are from 2 to 3 inches in length, and the nodes rather prominent. The leaves are about 9 inches long, seldom more than half an inch broad, tapering finely to a very sharp point and to a petiole at the base. The secondary nerves are about four in number on either side of the midrib, and the tessellation is perhaps hardly quite so conspicuous nor the leaves so thick as in the type. The edges are serrated, but only partially so on one side. The secondary nerves, as in the type, are palpable to the touch, and give the leaf, especially on the under side, quite a rough feeling. The leaf sheaths are fringed at the top. This species being so slender naturally in a measure loses the erect character which is such a feature in the type.

This plant is the TAIMIN-CHIKU of the Japanese, and is sent out by the French nurserymen as BAMBUSA GRAMINEA. The latter do not consider it hardy. Here, like the type, it was cut down by the winter of 1895, but is flourishing again gaily, and seems even more inclined to spread than its mate. The identity with the ARUNDINARIA HINDSII of Munro was determined at Kew by comparison with the dried specimens in the herbarium.

BAMBUSA PYGMÆA

WHEN one looks back upon the giant Bamboos of the Tropics it is difficult to believe that this pigmy is any relation of those monster grasses. The culms are from 6 inches to a foot, or a little more, in length. They are bright green in colour, but purple and flattened at the top, very slender, round, and with an extremely diminutive pipe, slightly zigzagged from knot to knot. The nodes are purple, prominent, and furnished with a protective band of waxy bloom round the base. The inter-nodes are sometimes rather over an inch long. The sheaths have a small arched ligule, armed with very minute hairs, and a tiny limbus. I fail to detect any tessellation in either sheath or limbus. The branches, which are borne singly or in pairs on the nodes, are very long in proportion to the size of the stem, to which they give a false appearance of being many-branched. The leaves, which are sometimes as much as 5 inches long by three-quarters of an inch wide, are a brilliant green, very regularly tessellated, serrated on both edges; and the upper surface is bristling with little teeth, while the lower surface is covered with a soft felt-like down. Ending in a sharp point, the leaf is pinched in, a little more on one side than the other, about half an inch from the end. The lower end is rounded off and finishes in a well-defined petiole.

There are usually from three to five secondary nerves flanking the midrib.

Small as this Bamboo is, it is a most determined little vagabond, its rampant rhizomes forcing their way everywhere, especially where they are not wanted, and taking no denial. It is a most valuable plant for making a thick carpet in a wild place, defying all attacks of frost or weather, as happy in winter as in summer, gay and bright at all times of the year, and a deadly foe to weeds; but beware of it in a border, it invades everything and will soon crowd out less sturdy neighbours. I have even had to dig up a gravel path to get rid of it.

PHYLLOSTACHYS AUREA

I WAS at one time inclined to undervalue the ornamental merits of this Bamboo, which appeared to me to be rather stiff and lacking in that graceful elegance which is such a conspicuous attraction in most members of the family. It has converted me, however, by the great beauty of its foliage, which is so rich in a well-matured specimen, that I have been encouraged to plant large clumps of it. If, as I think should be the case, a name ought at any rate to be of some little help in distinguishing a species, the name of AUREA is singularly ill chosen; for there is nothing golden about this plant except the yellow stem, and that is not by any means a peculiar characteristic, but is found in most of the Phyllostachys group. The Japanese call it HÔRAI-CHIKU, "the Bamboo of Fairyland," or TAIBÔ-CHIKU, "the Phœnix Bamboo." I sometimes wonder whether Siebold gave it the name of AUREA as a sort of pun upon the sound of Hôrai. It is a far-fetched guess, I know, but it is difficult to imagine how any one could have called this the "Golden" Bamboo, without something more than its appearance to go upon.

In this country PHYLLOSTACHYS AUREA has straight and very erect culms, which grow close round the base of the plant giving it a false air of having cæspitous roots, whereas it has a true rhizome which in its own home runs freely, and is only kept in restraint by our unfriendly climate. It is seen to the greatest advantage when planted in large and bold masses; and although this is true of all Bamboos, it is especially the case with PHYLLOSTACHYS AUREA, which, owing to the habit above-mentioned, has, when put out as an individual plant by itself, too much of the shape of the birch rod of an old-fashioned dame's school in the kingdom of Brobdingnag. One distinguishing feature by which this Bamboo may always be recognised is the shortness of the internodes at the base of the stem. The first five or six nodes of each culm are placed close together. It occasionally happens that by some freak one of these internodes will be a little longer than the others, but where that is the case, the elongation is not continued in the joints immediately above it. They revert to the short condition of those below.

The strong resemblance between the foliage of PHYLLO-STACHYS AUREA and that of PHYLLOSTACHYS MITIS has led to some confusion between the two, but the above-mentioned characteristic formation of the internodes at the base of the culm is peculiar to P. AUREA, which again does not show the bent stems frequently found in P. MITIS. And a further evidence of the distinction of the species lies in the fact that P. AUREA is, in this country at any rate, far hardier and easier of cultivation than P. MITIS; and that the rhizomatous character of the rootstock is not so easily seen from the position of the culms in the former as in the latter. The leaves, too, are far more sharply serrated in P. AUREA than in P. MITIS. In a young state it is difficult to distinguish the two species, but as they grow older each puts forth its characteristic features and asserts its identity. Messrs. Rivière remark that, like as the two plants are in the early stages of their life, P. MITIS never degenerates into P. AUREA, nor does P. AUREA ever rise to the dignity of P. MITIS. With these differences, and bearing in mind the fact that P. AUREA is altogether a smaller species than P. MITIS, for the foliage and general appearance of P. AUREA the description of P. MITIS will suffice, and avoid vain repetition. The colour of the bud scales is somewhat variable, light green, tipped with pink or brown edging, never so dark as in P. MITIS.

In Lord de Saumarez's garden at Shrubland PHYLLO-STACHYS AUREA is 14 feet 6 inches high, the canes being 2¾ inches round.

In the year 1893 a Bamboo was received here and at Kew from Japan under the name of BAMBUSA STERILIS, which the Japanese Gardeners' Association describe as closely allied to PHYLLOSTACHYS HETEROCYCLA. This appears to me to be undistinguishable from PHYLLOSTACHYS AUREA, and the authorities at Kew confirm that opinion. Curiously enough, the plants were covered with an undeveloped inflorescence, which proved to be infested with a hitherto undescribed ergot.

PHYLLOSTACHYS MITIS

In pride of stature this is the noblest of all the Bamboos
generally cultivated in this country. At Shrubland the
culms of plants imported some eight years ago have reached
a height of 19 feet 5 inches and are 4½ inches in circumference.
In its native countries (China and Japan) it grows as high
as 60 feet. The stems, which generally spring straight out
of the ground like spears, are, when fully developed, beautifully arched, and have for that reason a grace which is not
to be found in PHYLLOSTACHYS AUREA ; sometimes, however,
—and this is a very marked characteristic of the species
which I have observed in no other—the culms instead of
being straight are curved shortly after leaving the ground,
but usually bend back again after some considerable growth
has been made, so that the tips are ultimately in the same
axis as the point of deviation. I have already attempted to
describe the growth of PHYLLOSTACHYS MITIS, observing how
the young shoots when they first appear above ground seem
to hang fire for a while before taking their upward flight.
When once they start, they are drawn up with great rapidity,
growing even in this country as much as 6 inches or more in
the twenty-four hours ; the utmost growth that I have myself
observed in the same space of time being 4½ inches, but

mine are young plants. Messrs. Rivière have made most
interesting experiments on the growth of Bamboos, of which
they give tables. The maximum growth of an adult plant
of PHYLLOSTACHYS MITIS during twenty-four hours in
Algiers was 20 inches! They note that PHYLLOSTACHYS
MITIS makes its chief growth during the night, whereas
the other plants of similar habit, such as P. VIRIDI-GLAU-
CESCENS, AUREA, NIGRA, etc., grow fastest under the influence
of sunlight and are more sluggish at night. The marvellous
power of growth which Bamboos possess is shown by the
fact that in Bengal BAMBUSA TULDA has been known to grow
as much as three centimètres (upwards of 1¼ inch) during an
hour!

PHYLLOSTACHYS MITIS shows in a marked degree all those
features which are characteristic of the family to which it
belongs. In a mature stem for the first few feet from the
ground the internodes are round, for the lower nodes being
barren of branches there is no pressure of the bud under the
sheath to cause the groove with its two depressions which
on the higher internodes leave the impress of two twin
branches—the one short, the other long—their two beds in the
groove being marked by a distinct ridge. If there be a third
branchlet it is but an embryo, and generally disappears as
soon as it is developed. The sheaths enwrap the culm in all
its length until it is nearly developed, when the lower branches
first set the example of starting out and throwing off their
guardians. Gradually all the sheaths are forced away, and
the stem is clothed from top to toe in its graceful frondage.
The sheaths are tessellated, ending in a narrow fringed ligule
with a limbus, which, varying much in size, is narrow and

lanceolated, often variegated with yellow or orange stripes. The outer surface of the sheaths, which is of a brownish colour, is apt to be splashed with purplish spots, but these are not nearly so strongly marked as in Phyllostachys Quiliol When the withered sheaths drop off, the deep green stem, shining like enamel, gradually ripens into a bright yellow colour like golden corn. The axillary bud scales are a shining brown. The foliage is very beautiful, especially in a two-year-old culm, when the branchlets clothe it with a dense and brilliant green leafage, which, stirred by the wind, shows the blue tinge of the lower face of the leaf, producing a most pleasing effect. The leaves are by no means uniform in size; some are quite small—not much more than 1 inch long—whereas others (generally the terminal leaves of branches) are some 6 inches in length by 1 inch in breadth. Such a leaf will show some six or seven secondary nerves flanking the midrib,—the number of secondary nerves being in proportion to the size of the leaf. The shape is lanceolate, tapering to a very fine point, and ending at the base in a well-defined petiole. One edge is serrated, the other almost smooth, but the serration is not so sharp as in Phyllostachys Aurea. The leaf sheaths, which end in an elongated ligule, are fringed at the insertion of the leaf with a number of rather coarse hairs.

The underground procession of the rhizome is much more marked than in Phyllostachys Aurea, the stems appearing on alternate sides along its course, which they very distinctly indicate, although the running powers in this country are of course very poor, compared with what they are in hotter climates. Whereas in Phyllostachys Aurea

the rootstock is so checked back, that one might almost
believe the plant to be cæspitous did one not know that
it is not so,—in PHYLLOSTACHYS MITIS the rhizomatous
character, though stunted, is well maintained in appearance
as well as in fact.

In China and Japan the young shoots of this Bamboo are
eaten, some gastronomers professing to detect in them the
flavour of asparagus. This, I confess, demands some faith.
The consistency is crisp and pleasant, like that of celery, but
the flavour depends upon the sauce—at least that is my
experience. To its culinary merits, such as they are, the
plant owes the synonym EDULIS, which is at any rate a less
foolish name than MITIS. The Japanese name is MÔSÔ-CHIKU,
the Noble Bamboo, from two Chinese words signifying a
"superior clan" or "kindred."

One word of caution in regard to PHYLLOSTACHYS MITIS
I feel bound to add. It is certainly not so hardy as many
of its congeners. I have made inquiries in many quarters
as to its behaviour during last winter,[1] and all the answers
that I have received bear out my own experience. Most of
the tallest culms were cut down to the ground, and although
the roots and even some stems remained alive, yet the
plants received a severe shock, and the growth of the
summer of 1895 was distinctly less than that of preceding seasons. Plants that had been established for some
years suffered apparently as much as younger specimens,
and it will probably take two or three propitious seasons
to restore them to their former beauty. We may hope
that such a winter—a record of disasters to plant life—

[1] The winter of 1895, when the thermometer in many places fell below zero.

may not soon occur again. But it will be well to learn a
lesson of caution as to those plants to which it proved
most pernicious, and at any rate, not to place them in
exposed situations. Among these must certainly be reckoned
PHYLLOSTACHYS MITIS.

PHYLLOSTACHYS SULPHUREA

A HANDSOME golden-stemmed Bamboo, which in appearance has a great affinity with PHYLLOSTACHYS MITIS, though Messrs. Rivière see a connection between it and PHYLLO-STACHYS FLEXUOSA. It is far stiffer, and has less active roots than P. FLEXUOSA; while the only differences which I can detect between it and P. MITIS are (1) that it is inferior in stature; (2) that the stem is, if anything, rather more brilliantly coloured, and (3) that the leaves are more sharply serrated. In this latter respect P. SULPHUREA seems to hold a middle place between P. MITIS and P. AUREA, the teeth being more palpable than in the former, and less so than they are in the latter. In other respects the characteristics are indentical; indeed I doubt whether there are many experts who would back themselves to distinguish between P. SULPHUREA and a specimen of P. MITIS of equal size. In hardihood P. SULPHUREA is far superior to P. MITIS. Last winter (1895), which played sad havoc with the one, left the other practically unharmed.

The Shrubland plants have attained a height of 13 feet with a circumference of 2¼ inches round the stem.

IN the Comedy of Errors that our Bamboos have been made to play PHYLLOSTACHYS QUILIOI may almost claim to have acted the chief part. Antipholus of Syracuse was not more like his brother of Ephesus than, according to some writers, this Phyllostachys is to MITIS; others would have it that the resemblance is to AUREA, while a third authority was for some time convinced that P. QUILIOI, VIRIDI-GLAUCESCENS, and FLEXUOSA were one and the same plant. However, I think that it is now pretty well decided that not only are they all quite distinct, but that P. QUILIOI may more especially be pointed to as having characteristics which are altogether its own. The mistake arose from the ignorance of those who a few years ago were sending out the plants. In one garden I know that QUILIOI was grown as and labelled MITIS; while the owner, having sent to a distinguished foreign nurseryman for QUILIOI, VIRIDI-GLAUCESCENS, and FLEXUOSA, received a consignment of plants, purporting to be the three species asked for, but every one of which turned out to be VIRIDI-GLAUCESCENS. Was it to be wondered at that the Socinian heresy should be deeply rooted in that garden? In vain the owner strained his eyes, searching with inquisitive lens for differences which did not exist. PHYLLO-

STACHYS VIRIDI-GLAUCESCENS being for ever compared with itself,—

> These two Antipholuses, these two so like,
> And these two Dromios, one in semblance,

were enough to addle the brain of the wisest Duke that ever administered the law in Ephesus.

As a matter of fact PHYLLOSTACHYS QUILIOI is a tall bold Bamboo of noble aspect and quite unlike any of its congeners. At Shrubland the culms have reached a height of 18 feet 6 inches with a circumference of 3¾ inches. The plant has a far looser habit than either P. MITIS or P. AUREA, the stems being gracefully arched though hardly as lissome as those of P. VIRIDI-GLAUCESCENS and P. FLEXUOSA. The rhizome, though not quite so active as it is in the two latter species, runs far more freely in this country than that of P. MITIS or P. AUREA. A distinctive feature in the species is the great length of the branches in proportion to the height of the culm, which gives a spreading appearance to the frondage. The leaves are much larger than they are in the other members of the Phyllostachys group, though they vary considerably in size. In a portion of a stem before me some are as much as 8 inches in length by an inch and three-quarters in width ; others are but 2 inches long, but the breadth is far greater in proportion than is to be found in other species. In the larger leaves there are from seven to eight secondary nerves on each side of the midrib. The serration of one edge of the leaf is very conspicuous. In some cases it is sharp on both edges; it is altogether different from the same feature in P. MITIS, AUREA, etc. Nor is the colour less distinct, being a dark green often spotted with brown, the lower face very glaucous. The petiole is relatively long and well defined, springing from a rounded base, while the sharp point is much curved to one side. The leaf sheaths, which are purple at the tips, are fringed with a quantity of coarse, long, bristly hairs. The ligule is long and rounded.

The sheaths which envelop the culm form one of the most peculiar features of the species. They are of a pinkish brown colour deeply mottled with purple spots, such as are sometimes found in the sheaths of P. MITIS, but far more intense. The ligule is not very conspicuous, the limbus long, narrow, and dark in colour. As the sheaths fall, pushed aside by the branches, they reveal a most brilliantly polished dark green stem with very salient knots stained with purple. The two branches grow with great rapidity, the longer one reaching three times the length of the internode within the groove of which it was once so tightly imprisoned.

The bud scales are green at the base, pinkish brown round the edges.

I think I have pointed out sufficient characters to show cause why PHYLLOSTACHYS QUILIOI should be considered a distinct species. To me it is a Bamboo to be recognised among a thousand, and I have shown it now to many distinguished botanists who have, without exception, adopted the same view.

P. QUILIOI is also known by the synonym MAZELI after M. Mazel, in whose garden near Anduze (Gard) it has, according to Messrs. Rivière, attained noble proportions. The name QUILIOI was given to commemorate its first introduction into Europe in the year 1866 by the French Admiral, Du Quilio, who brought it from Japan.

PHYLLOSTACHYS VIRIDI-GLAUCESCENS

THOSE who are responsible for naming many of our Bamboos have certainly shown poverty of invention and a feeble measure of discrimination. Here is another species flaunting a name which would seem to point to a prominent character peculiar to itself, and distinguishing it from its kith and kin, whereas this character is no peculiarity at all, but a matter of common property in which the whole family has a share. It is true that the foliage is of a radiant green; equally true that when a passing breeze stirs the leaves the glaucous colour of their lower face is revealed in charming contrast, and a chameleon-like change takes place; but PHYLLOSTACHYS VIRIDI-GLAUCESCENS has no monopoly of this brilliant, almost iridescent effect,—which is the heritage of well-nigh every Bamboo with which we are acquainted,—and is not even the one in which it is the most conspicuous. To the injudicious application of such names as this, setting up on behalf of one individual exclusive claims to rights which belong to the many, may be attributed much of the confusion of which we have been the victims.

Be that as it may, there the name is, and it must stand. At any rate it is certain that we have here not only a hardy Bamboo which has held its own without flinching against the rudest buffets of our climate, but also one of striking loveliness both in colour and form. Indeed there are some competent judges who would crown it Queen of Beauty. To this length I cannot go. For my taste, the growth is a little too straggling, and I prefer the statelier yet equally elegant curves of PHYLLOSTACHYS HENONIS and P. BORYANA. The Queen of Beauty should have a perfect figure. Yet would I not be held to undervalue the merits of P. VIRIDI-GLAUCESCENS. Paris no doubt recognised to the full the awe-striking majesty of Here, and the colder loveliness of Pallas Athene, though the meed of fairest fell to the divine witchery of Aphrodite. If a spell has been cast upon me by the magic beauty of P. HENONIS I am not insensible to the fascination of the rival beauties.

In a mature clump of PHYLLOSTACHYS VIRIDI-GLAUCESCENS the stems which spring from the centre of the plant, being supported by one another, are tall, slender, and upright, though much zigzagged, bending gracefully outwards on all sides. Those which are on the outside seem to grow horizontally, for, lacking support, they are borne down by the weight of their own foliage, though that is hardly quite as luxuriant as it is in some species. This gives the plant the rather weak and straggling appearance of which I, perhaps in a hypercritical mood, have complained above.

The colour of the culms is at first a bright green, which as they ripen fades into a rather dingy yellow. The lower rim of the salient, violet-tinted node is in the early state white, and underneath it for about half an inch down the stem is a thin layer of waxy bloom. With age the white rim disappears and the whole of the knot, but especially the

lower part, assumes an olive green colour darker than the
rest of the stem. The branches are very long in proportion
to the internode, and the third branchlet, which in the other
species of the Phyllostachys group is so generally wanting,
or, if present, disappears, is more apt to be persistent.
The groove left by the pressure of the branches appears
to be often almost flat, but the double channel is well
defined.

The ligule of the culm sheath when fully developed and
ready to drop off is worthy of careful examination, for it
shows a character which is one of the chief aids in distinguishing the species from PHYLLOSTACHYS FLEXUOSA,
which it so much resembles as to have at one time deceived
the very elect. In P. VIRIDI-GLAUCESCENS the ligule of the
sheath is continued on either side of the limbus in two little
fringed ears, which are not found in P. FLEXUOSA. Other
distinguishing features are to be found in the bud scales
which in the latter species are tipped with pink, whereas in
the former they are of a pale green, and in the colour of
the nodes of the culm which are far less dark in P. FLEXUOSA,
and hardly show the violet colour which is so conspicuous in
P. VIRIDI-GLAUCESCENS. In the former, moreover, the third
branchlet is very rare.

As will have been gathered from what I have said above,
the frondage is rather loose, and the branches somewhat
scantily clothed when compared with some other Bamboos.
The leaves are lanceolate, ending in a fine point, tapering to
a well-defined petiole at the base, serrated all along one edge
and partially towards the point on the other. On either side
of the midrib are about five secondary nerves. The length is

from 3 to 4 inches—perhaps hardly as much—the width not much more than half an inch; the colour a bright cheerful green on the upper face, glaucous on the lower. The leaf sheaths are of a purplish colour, fringed at the insertion of the leaves with hairs on the sides of an elongated ligule.

The rootstock is extremely active, and when once well established the plant spreads rapidly, new culms appearing at some distance from the parent stock.

The culms have grown to a height of 18 feet at Shrub-land and nearly 15 feet at Kew, with a circumference of no more than 2 inches. They are very hollow and as a consequence extremely brittle and apt to split. A stem 11 feet high and nearly 2 inches in circumference has a pipe about three-eighths of an inch in diameter, the wall measuring only one-eighth of an inch.

The species is perfectly hardy when once established, and has stood uninjured through our severest winter. Yet it is necessary to be cautious in planting it out after travelling. I have lost a good many plants by over great confidence in this respect. Newly arrived plants should be carefully potted and remain for their first winter under the protection of a temperate house, according to the recommendations given in my general remarks upon Culture.

Thus, to the best of my ability, I have endeavoured to point out the leading features of this pretty Bamboo as they appear in this country. In warmer climates, according to Messrs. Rivière, the plant has a very different aspect. The culms are stouter, straighter, and rounder, the internodes are longer, the knots more pronounced, and the third branchlet, which is so common in the north, is abortive, owing to the

K

great rapidity of growth.   The colour of the two-year-old
stems is a bright yellow, the upper rim of the knots is a
darker yellow, while the lower rim is of a grayish colour, the
white band of waxy bloom under the node being most conspicuous.

The species was first introduced into Europe from the
north of China about the year 1846 by the French Vice-
Admiral, Count Cécille.

PHYLLOSTACHYS FLEXUOSA

AT first sight it is certainly not easy to distinguish this species from the preceding one. There are, however, marked points of difference to which I have called attention under the description of PHYLLOSTACHYS VIRIDI-GLAUCESCENS, and which therefore I need not recapitulate here. With me, moreover, this species has not in five years attained more than half the height reached by P. VIRIDI-GLAUCESCENS in the same period. The growth appears to be more compact, while the leaves are if anything smaller, but clothing the branches more densely.

Though the differences which I have described require, it must be admitted, some closeness of observation to detect, yet they are sufficient to establish the distinct nature of the two plants. But if they are not enough for that purpose there remains an arrow in the quiver which cannot but hit the mark. In the year 1876 P. FLEXUOSA flowered and fruited in the garden of the Hamma at Algiers, and in the gardens of Messrs. Thibaut and Keteleer at Sceaux, in France. Now Messrs. Rivière point out, and so far as I can ascertain the remark still holds good, the flower of P. VIRIDI-GLAUCESCENS has not yet been observed. The evidence is conclusive.

I venture to take from Messrs. Rivière the following

account of the flowering of PHYLLOSTACHYS FLEXUOSA, the
only one of this group of Bamboos upon which it has been
hitherto found.

The flowers are borne upon all the branches of the culms,
taking the place of leaves. They are grouped in a kind of
panicle, of which each division taken by itself represents a
spike of from 3 .to 4 centimètres in length, composed of
from eight to ten spikelets (sometimes fewer, sometimes as
many as fourteen) each bearing one, two, or very rarely three
flowers.

On each spike are found abortive flowers, fertile flowers,
and sterile flowers, the two latter generally together on the
same spikelet. At the base of the back of the spike and
attached to the axis which supports it is a minute keel-
shaped glume or scale, with an obtuse top and slightly downy
on the outside. From the centre of this persistent organ,
hardly a millimètre in height, the spike rises. At the base
of the latter are six scaly sheaths ; the three first are very
small and short, not more than from 1 to 4 millimètres
in length. Their summit is obtuse and emarginate, or rather
split from top to bottom. The three other sheaths are larger,
from 5 to 7 millimètres in length. One of them, the shortest,
has an obtuse summit, but the other two present different
characters. They end in a small fringed membrane, very
slightly developed, a ligule in miniature with a very short
limbus. On one side, and on part of the other, the sheaths
are edged with small whitish hairs. Each of these differently
shaped sheaths is accompanied by a very minute bud, more
or less developed, often only in a rudimentary condition, and
which from its position remains in embryo, the scaly sheaths

with their bud representing spikelets of which the flowers
are altogether abortive. After these first abortive spikelets
come the fertile spikelets composed as follows :—

1. A scaly sheath, 20 to 25 millimètres in length with a
width, when spread out, of from 5 to 7 millimètres, ending in
a little pointed tongue. Between this last organ and the
end of the sheath is a very short slightly-ciliated ligule; the
upper face of the sheath is a little rough to the touch. On the
whole of one edge and part of the other are tiny whitish hairs.

2. At the base of this sheath a small keel-shaped bract
from 5 to 8 millimètres in length, thin, soft, whitish, almost
obtuse with the dorsal part slightly hairy. At the base is
a very small bud, hardly developed, which represents no
doubt another abortive flower.

3. Above this keel-shaped bract a membranous glume or
scale about 15 millimètres in length, soft and ending in a
short point. A few silky hairs are seen on the edges towards
the extremity of the scale, the dorsal part of which is slightly
downy.

4. A glume or scale of a different nature 20 to 25
millimètres in length with a very fine point, thicker, tougher,
and longer than the membranous scale, and smooth.

5. A last scale, similar in form to the preceding one, but
differing from it in that its point is invariably split in two
for part of its length.

These five organs composing the spikelet are distichous,
imbricated, and rolled the one over the other, especially the
two last. Their colour is green at the base, tinged with
violet towards the extremity, notably in those parts which
are exposed to the action of light.

6. At the base of the dorsal part of the last scale, which is at the end of the spikelet and inserted on the same plane, is a small filiform awn, sometimes of the same length as the scale, generally only half that length.

7. On the top of the spikelet, at the base of the last scale and enveloped by it, are the reproductive organs consisting of the stamens and pistil. When the latter have reached their full development, they lengthen out and escape from the opening of their enveloping scales which represent a sort of case or scabbard.

The stamens, which are three in number, are inserted at the base of and around the ovary. They are very long, from 25 to 35 millimètres, and the lower half of the length is imprisoned within the scales which constitute the flower. The filament of each stamen is white and of extreme slenderness. The anthers are much developed, 10 to 12 millimètres in length, pale yellow, and hanging by the emarginate portion of one extremity. They have two cells. When their development is complete and the pollen is about to escape they open from the top, but only along a portion of their length.

The ovary is relatively very small, globular-ovoid in shape.

The style is placed on the top of the ovary; it is of the same length as the scales. The stigma is trifid, feathered, and violet in colour, expanding as it leaves its envelopes. The violet tint of the stigma is seen along a portion of the style.

Here, then, is a fertile, single-flowered spikelet with the reproductive organs united at the base of the topmost scale, indicating a species with hermaphrodite flowers.

A second form of spikelet with two flowers, the one sterile, the other fertile, is composed of a sheath with ligule and limbus enfolding the two flowers at their base, and of a keel-shaped scale at the base of which is developed the sterile flower. This latter is composed (1) of a membranous scale; (2) of a longer and more pointed scale; (3) of a scale similar to the last, but with its point split along part of its length; (4) of the reproductive organs in a condition of malformation. The fertile flower is placed a little above the sterile flower. It is composed (1) of a membranous scale; (2) of a pointed scale; (3) of a scale with the point split; (4) of the reproductive organs perfectly formed and developed.

Another form of spikelet is found, single-flowered and fertile, but lacking one organ in the shape of the keel-shaped scale.

There is yet one spikelet to be examined. It is terminal, placed at the end of the spike, and differing from the others. It is composed of four parts only: (1) a sheath with ligule and limbus; (2) a pointed scale; (3) a scale with the point split; (4) the reproductive organs entire and perfect. The keel-shaped scale and the membranous scale are wanting.

On some spikes spikelets have been found, fertile and single-flowered, with six floral envelopes instead of five. In such cases there are two membranous scales instead of one.

Rarely spikelets are found with three flowers—two sterile and one fertile—and in some cases spikelets with two flowers, both being fertile and fully developed.

During the progress of growth the organs composing the spike are green, tinged with violet, but as soon as the inflorescence is developed and the stamens are set free, the

violet colour disappears almost entirely; the scaly leaves at
the base of the spike turn yellow, while some of them are
detached and fall off. In shape the spike is elliptical and
slightly arched. The ligulated sheaths are distichous as we
have seen, but during this period of vegetation they are so
turned that their extremities close in towards the dorsal part
of the spike, giving the latter the appearance of being
one sided.

The first sign of approaching inflorescence is given by
the leaves turning yellow, withering, and falling off. When
they have entirely disappeared the flowers begin to show
themselves. For some time before their complete development, two of the three stamens are lodged side by side in the
topmost scale, while the third lives in solitude in the one
immediately below it.

Messrs. Rivière remark that in the flowers of PHYLLO-
STACHYS FLEXUOSA glumellæ are of extremely rare occurrence,
indeed in the many specimens that they have examined
they have only found them once.

During the period of flowering the culms are completely
bare of leaves, and, with the ripening of the fruit, vegetation
ceases, although occasionally the branches produce at their
points a few abortive floral organs. As the culms disappear
small shoots rise up bearing flowers, which are sometimes
perfect and sometimes abortive. In other cases the little
culms bearing leaves and flowers together live for a period
and are succeeded by others bearing leaves only and of
stronger growth. Thus it seems that the rhizomes are not
altogether killed after flowering, but, though greatly enfeebled,
gradually show signs of returning life and vigour.

I trust that I may be forgiven for borrowing in so barefaced a manner from Messrs. Rivière. It has been their good fortune to fall in with an unique experience, which their talent and knowledge have enabled them to describe with singularly lucid felicity; but, unfortunately, their book is not available to all English lovers of Bamboos, upon whom I was anxious that so interesting an observation should not be lost. Above all, I would call special attention to the vitality of the plant after flowering as evidence in favour of the opinion that the rhizomes are not in all cases killed by the process.

For horticultural purposes PHYLLOSTACHYS FLEXUOSA may be described as an ornamental Bamboo of neat and compact habit; not a dwarf, yet far smaller than most of its congeners; presenting all the characteristics of the Phyllostachys group—a slightly zigzagged, gracefully arching stem, bearing at the nodes two branches, one long and one short, not more flexible—maugre its name—than others of the genus. The colour of the stem is bright green, fading as it ripens into a dull greenish yellow. The scale buds resemble those of P. AUREA. The foliage is hardly to be distinguished from that of P. VIRIDI-GLAUCESCENS. The culm sheaths, however, differ materially from those of that species in lacking the little ear-like membranes which the latter exhibit on either side of the ligule flanking the limbus. The rhizome is fairly active, though not so rampant as in P. VIRIDI-GLAUCESCENS. This moderation of behaviour as regards invading the territory of other plants, combined with a stature which is hardly likely to exceed 8 feet in this country, 3 mètres being its height in warmer climates, render P. FLEXUOSA a valuable

acquisition for those who have not space to spare for the
larger species.   At Leonardslee the culms are 6 feet 10
inches high, 1 inch in circumference.

As to its hardihood there is no room for doubt.   It was
introduced into Europe from the colder regions of China by
the French Société d'Acclimatation in the year 1864.   Not
to be confounded with the BAMBUSA FLEXUOSA, a spinose non-
hardy species from Canton, described by Munro.

PHYLLOSTACHYS VIOLESCENS

THERE are some authorities who regard this as a variety of
PHYLLOSTACHYS VIRIDI-GLAUCESCENS, but inasmuch as the
flower and fruit of neither has come under observation, and
there are certainly marked differences in the appearance
and hardihood of the two, their opinion must be considered
as a mere surmise, unsupported by evidence. The one point
of similarity which I can detect in both is the frequent
occurrence at each node of the third branchlet, which in
most species is generally abortive or absent.

If this beautiful Bamboo added hardihood to its other
merits it would indeed be a garden treasure. Unfortunately
the last two winters have handled it very roughly, the foliage
being stripped and often the culms themselves being cut
back. I fear it is but a fair-weather friend. Still the
rhizomes have been uninjured in spite of the mischief, and
their great activity has been shown by new culms shooting
up all round the plants and often a yard or more away
from them. Some cultivators recommend cutting back the
canes every year. I should prefer trusting to time for the
acclimatisation of the species. Already I cannot help
fancying that I see signs of a hardier generation of culms
than those which were first produced, and I do not despair

of success. The roots are sturdy and vigorous, and every
year as the plants are better established the culms are
produced earlier in the season, so that they have more time
to ripen their wood, and thus gain powers of resistance.

The canes, the growth of which does not vary in manner
from those of the other species of the Phyllostachys group,
are of a deep violet, almost black, colour during the first year
of their growth. This with the violet sheaths of the branches
has given the name to the species. But this peculiar colour
is not persistent. As the cane ripens it changes to a dull,
dingy yellow or brown, exactly reversing the order of things
to be observed in PHYLLOSTACHYS NIGRA where the culms,
green in their first year, ripen into a beautiful glossy black
in the second.

The leaves vary greatly in size. I have two before me.
The one is 7 inches long by nearly 2 inches broad, the other
is but 2 inches by half an inch. The one has eight secondary
nerves on each side of the midrib, the other but three. It is
noteworthy that the larger leaves in all these Bamboos are
found upon young shoots or upon the ends of the lower
branches near the ground. The foliage on the tall mature
stems more rarely shows great differences in size. The leaves
are lanceolate, ending in a fine point at the top, and in a
well-pronounced purplish petiole at the base. They are
sharply serrated more or less on both edges. The leaf
sheaths, which have a long, rounded, and fringed ligule,
bear at the insertion of the leaf a cluster of coarse purple
hairs. In colour the foliage is a dark green on the upper
face with a beautiful glaucous tint on the lower. The culm
sheaths are of a purplish brown colour, with a strongly-

marked ligule, convex at the top and fringed. The limbus is narrow, varying in length, a dark brownish green in colour. As in all the members of the Phyllostachys family, the culm sheaths are early pushed aside by the branches, wither and fall off.

At Shrubland the plants are 13 feet high with a circumference of 2 inches.

PHYLLOSTACHYS NIGRA

ALL sun-worshippers, who wing their flight southward with
the swallows, know the Black Bamboo as one of the chief
ornaments which grace the gardens of the Riviera. Indeed it
has been long established even in this less genial climate, for
Loudon in the second edition of his *Arboretum et Fruticetum*,
published in 1854, mentions it as having been for some ten
or twelve years growing in the Horticultural Society's gardens,
so that it is a wonder that it should not have become a less
rare feature with us than it is; the more so in that it is
perfectly hardy and, in a fairly favourable situation, flourishes
with great vigour. At Leonardslee the culms are 20 feet
high with a circumference of all but 3 inches, but this must
be regarded as very exceptional. At Shrubland and at Kew
they are 10 feet high with a circumference of 2 inches. I
find it a little capricious and difficult to establish unless the
precautions which I have so many times indicated are taken;
but with common care all trouble disappears, and, once it
has taken hold of the ground, no Bamboo is hardier: our
rudest winters seem powerless to injure it. Yet if, instead
of being one of the easiest, it were one of the most difficult
exotics to train to our will, it would still be well worth the
pains taken, for it is almost impossible to exaggerate the

PHYLLOSTACHYS NIGRA

worth of those qualities which give it a patent of nobility in
the plant world. And if it be shown in a position where the
black stem, contrasting so finely with the dark green and
glaucous shimmering of the leaves, is well brought into view,
lording it over a fairy court of Solomon's Seal, Foxglove, tall
Ferns, Loosestrife, and such like woodland beauties whose
name is legion, each enhancing the other, its loveliness is
made for memory.

Both in the greenhouse and in the open this Bamboo has
each year been the first with me to show signs of growth,
and by the middle of April I have generally found piercing
the ground many little brown cones, fringed with white hairs
and tipped with tiny green tongues. Slowly at first, and
gradually faster, the culm sheaths enfolding one another are
drawn up until the full height has been reached, when the
twin branches, rejecting their protectors, force them aside,
and the olive green stem, darkest under the nodes, is revealed,
slightly zigzagged, tapering to a gracefully bending point.
The nodes are a conspicuous feature ; the upper rim is deep
black, the lower rim edged with white. In the second year
the colour of the culm changes to the characteristic glossy
black from which the species takes its name. The culm
sheaths are rather thick and dark in colour, with a few easily-
distinguished cross veins. The upper side of the edges,
which overlap one another for most of their length, is fringed
with hairs—a protection against water which is not necessary
where the sheaths completely encircle the stem. The ligule is
well defined, darker in colour than the rest of the sheath, and
much fringed. The limbus, which varies in size, lengthening
on the upper parts of the stem, is serrated, narrow, rather

waving, and pointed. On each side of the limbus is seen as
in PHYLLOSTACHYS VIRIDI-GLAUCESCENS a small hairy membrane; but this feature is not invariable. The sheaths and
all their parts quickly wither and fall off. Under the sheaths
the branches, before bursting out, are imprisoned in a small
scale deeply cut into two hairy, fringed lobes. The leaf
sheaths, as distinguished from the culm sheaths, are very
thin and short-lived. The ligule is deep and round, the
limbus very small. The bud scales are dark and mottled
with black.

As the lower nodes of P. NIGRA are barren of branches,
the internodes on that part of the stem are round and do
not show the double groove which is found upon the higher
and branch-bearing portion.

Munro says, "The stems, although slender, are nearly
solid, and appear to be generally used for such purposes as
require great strength and toughness"; and, quoting Miquel,
who says that this Bamboo seems to come very near to
Bambusa stricta of Roxburgh, the solid so-called "male
Bamboo" of which lances are made in India, he goes on to
remark that he cannot understand this unless it has reference
to the culms being nearly solid. Moreover, he describes the
species as "culmo superne nigrescente, subsolido." This is
altogether wrong. It is true that the wood is tougher than
it is in many Bamboos and does not split so easily, but, as
a matter of fact, it is an extremely hollow cane, a stem less
than half an inch in diameter showing a pipe five-sixteenths
of an inch across.

The leaves, which are linear-lanceolate, are pointed at the
top, and rounded at the base, or attenuated into a short

petiole ; serrated more or less on both edges, narrow, varying
in size from 2 to 6 inches in length, the longest and largest
being found as usual on the scrubby growth at the base of
the plant.   Munro says : " The leaves in this species are much
thinner than in any other of the genus ; and although they
vary much as to pubescence, the midrib is invariably hairy
on the under side towards the base, as is the case in ARUNDI-
NARIA FALCATA." The midrib is flanked by from three to
seven secondary nerves.

The rhizome does not penetrate the ground to any great
depth, but remains near the surface, sometimes shooting
upwards to avoid some obstacle and then bending downward
again, forming a distinct hoop or arch above ground. It is
the rhizome of PHYLLOSTACHYS NIGRA which furnishes the
tough and flexible Wang-hai cane of commerce, which I have
already described as typical of the underground stems of this
group of Bamboos.

Messrs. Rivière make PHYLLOSTACHYS NIGRA a native of
the East Indies. This is a mistake. The plant is indigenous
in China and Japan, and it has been referred to India much
in the same way as Chinese porcelain which connoisseurs,
by the strangest of all blundering name-jumbles, used to call
" Indian China ! "   I rather doubt, indeed, whether there be
among the Bamboos of India any species which resembles
this Chinese and Japanese group of the Phyllostachides, for
the Indian species are described as caespitose, whereas a
leading feature of the Chinese and Japanese species, with
the exception of P. BAMBUSOIDES, is the rhizome with its
vagrant propensities, which, however they may be restrained
under our skies, are rampant in their native climate.

PHYLLOSTACHYS NIGRO-PUNCTATA

A FORM of PHYLLOSTACHYS NIGRA supposed to be rather
taller and more free-growing than the type. The stems,
instead of turning to a deep glossy black in their second year,
assume a brown colour speckled all over with darker spots.
There is no other character to differentiate it from P. NIGRA ;
indeed I much doubt whether there is any warranty for
keeping the two as separate species, rather, as it seems to
me, is P. NIGRO-PUNCTATA simply an accidental variation.
It is, however, hardier than the type, which makes me think
that it may be P. NIGRA brought from a colder home than
the blacker variety, where the sun has not been strong
enough to bring out the full colour. Although I have
planted out a great many specimens without giving them the
slightest protection, exposing them immediately after their
arrival from abroad in places at the mercy of our bleakest
winds, I have not lost a single one. In cases where the type
was treated in the same way I lost a large percentage. With
care, however, this is unnecessary, and I should always
prefer planting the type, the colour of the culms being so
much more attractive.

PHYLLOSTACHYS BORYANA

THIS beautiful species is considered to be, like P. NIGRO-PUNCTATA, a variety of PHYLLOSTACHYS NIGRA. It is larger and bolder than either of the other two species (if, indeed, they may be reckoned as separate species), and is one of the handsomest and most vigorous of all the hardy Bamboos ; indeed I should place it with P. HENONIS and P. VIRIDI-GLAUCESCENS in the very front rank for beauty and elegance. They are the three Graces. The culms in this Bamboo differ from those of the type, and of PHYLLOSTACHYS NIGRO-PUNCTATA, in their colour, which, green at first, in their second season ripens into a rich yellow, duller than that of the culms of P. AUREA or P. MITIS, and splashed here and there with purplish brown blotches. The bud scales at the axils of the branches are very different from those of P. NIGRA and P. NIGRO-PUNCTATA, being of a pale yellowish green. The habit of the plant differs greatly from that of P. NIGRA and P. NIGRO-PUNCTATA, the branches being far longer in proportion to the length of the culm. Altogether, it is a puzzle to me why it should be accredited with such near relationship to species which it is so strangely unlike in many essential particulars. As regards hardihood, it is quite as trustworthy as P. NIGRO-PUNCTATA. I have never lost a plant, though my specimens have been anything but coddled. I have often found the rhizomes in this species running horizontally on the surface of the ground. When this is detected it is advisible to cover them with a little loose soil, and to keep them down with a light flat stone. This encourages the verticillate roots to strike downwards. Failing this precaution, I have known the rhizome to be killed back to the point where it left the earth, and the development of the plant to be to that extent retarded.

PHYLLOSTACHYS HENONIS

As I have already stated this is in my eyes the most beautiful member of a beautiful family. To describe justly a
favourite horse, a favourite dog, a favourite plant, is perhaps
what no man can do. He is bound to say too much, and too
little—too much to please others, too little to satisfy himself.
Besides enthusiasm is a deadly foe to accuracy. This much,
however, I have said before elsewhere, and I am prepared
to reassert without fear of contradiction, I regard PHYLLO-
STACHYS HENONIS as the embodiment of every grace to which
plant life is heir. In plant or in woman perfect health is
the best of all cosmetics, and perfect health PHYLLOSTACHYS
HENONIS has enjoyed under all the trials through which it
has passed during the last four years which have certainly
been most hostile. Droughty summers have not been able to
parch it ; ice-bound winters have failed to starve it ; and now,
in the month of January 1896, it is as green as at midsummer.
It had no protection, but was left to do battle with chill
December and the even deadlier blasts of March as best it
might, emerging from every engagement with renewed strength
and enhanced beauty. Many of its companions fell victims in
the unequal fight and sad voids were made in their ranks, but
in this battalion not so much as a single plume was laid low.

My plants, which have had four summers' growth, are 8 feet high. Their elders by a few years at Shrubland have grown to 14 feet, with a circumference in the culms of 1½ inch.

An 8-foot culm shows the following characteristics: The circumference is all but 1½ inch. The internodes are in length from 5 or 6 inches near the base and middle of the stem, lessening to 4 near the top. They are very distinctly grooved with the double furrow left by the pressure of the branches. The nodes, rimmed with dark blue green above and with a pale white below, are well defined. The colour is a bright green at first, ripening in the second year into a yellow rather less brilliant than in some species. The surface of the cane is rough to the touch. The wood is hard and tough, the cavity being about one-eighth of an inch in diameter, surrounded by walls of the same measurement in thickness. I find little or no trace of waxy bloom even under the nodes, where in other species it is most frequently seen. The culm sheaths have irregular transverse veinlets; the ligule is rather long; the limbus narrow. The culm sheath, bright green when it first encircles the newborn stem, soon withers to a dull straw colour, is pushed aside by the branches and, having served its purpose, disappears. As in P. viridi-glaucescens, there are frequently three branches on each node, or, at any rate, on many of the nodes. The longest branch measures 20 inches, the second 11, the third a little more than 6. The bud scales, which are the embryo branches and branchlets, are enamelled pale green. The linear-lanceolate leaves are borne in twos and threes on the ends of the purplish branchlets. Their colour is a brilliant

green on the upper face, while they show less glaucous colour
on the lower than is the case with most of the family. On
an adult stem they vary a little in size from about 2 to 3
inches in length by about three-eighths of an inch in width.
They taper to a very fine point, and are attenuated at the base
to a longer petiole than is usual among these Phyllostachides.
The tessellation is very distinct, close, and regular. The pale
midrib is well defined, flanked on either side by sometimes as
many as six or seven secondary nerves. One edge is markedly
serrated, in the other the teeth are rare or absent. The leaf
sheaths are inclined to be purple in colour, with a much-cut-
up ligule fringed at the insertion of the leaf with purple hairs.
The rootstock runs pretty freely even in this climate, and will
probably develop the power more strongly as the plants
mature themselves.

It is to its habit that PHYLLOSTACHYS HENONIS owes its
surpassing loveliness. The two-year-old culms, burthened
with the weight of their own leaves clustering in triplets
and borne upon innumerable branchlets, bend almost to the
earth in graceful curves, forming a groundwork of most
elegant beauty, from which the stems of the year spring up
in slight zigzag, arching over at the top and waving their
feathery fronds, the delicate green leaves seeming to float in
the air. It must be from this quality that it derives its
Japanese name HA-CHIKU, the two Chinese characters with
which it is written, signifying the "light or volatile Bamboo."

PHYLLOSTACHYS CASTILLONIS

IT is not always that rarity and beauty go hand in hand; when they are found together great is the joy of the collector. Such a combination is present in PHYLLOSTACHYS CASTILLONIS, for not only is it a very beautiful plant, but it is certainly uncommon, at any rate in European gardens. Though I found it advertised in plenty of catalogues, when sent for it was not forthcoming, and finally I had to import it from Japan. My plants have now three summers' growth upon them, and have gone through two exceptionally hard winters. In 1894, 24° of frost did them no harm, but the month of February 1895 cut some of them badly. The culms had not had sufficient sun to ripen them during the summer of 1894, and they suffered accordingly. The blazing heat, however, of the spring of 1895, continued through the dog-days, warmed them into life again, not a plant being lost, and now in January 1896 they are as bright as ever, though they have hardly made as much growth as might have been hoped for had they not received so severe a check. I think that, considering what they have gone through, and that, too, before they were fully established, we may fairly call them hardy. M. Marliac, who has a far longer experience of them than I have, tells me that the foliage suffers much in snow. This, however, is but a temporary evil at the worst, and I trust to see the species more generally introduced than it has been hitherto. It may be hoped, moreover, that such a winter as the last will not occur twice in a lifetime, and that hunters and Bamboos may not again be attacked with such persistent cruelty by that "Général Février," upon whom the Emperor Nicholas placed vain reliance in the days of the Crimean War.

Unique in this respect among its brethren of the Phyllostachys family, this species has both stem and leaves brilliantly variegated. It needs no elaborate description, for it stands out with an identity which is unmistakable. The stems, which with me have reached a height of from 5 to 6 feet, are thick in proportion to their height as compared with other Bamboos, being about 1 inch or rather more in circumference. They are as smooth as polished ivory, and much zigzagged from node to node. The wood is hard and tough; the cavity, in a stem of 1¼ inch in circumference, is three-sixteenths of an inch in diameter. The colouring of the stem is curious. The double groove is bright green, the rest of its circumference being yellow, and this colouring is not on the surface only but goes right through the wood to the cavity. Owing to their position the two colours are alternate all the way up the culm, the hues being intensified with age.

In the knots the upper rim, which is extremely prominent, is dark yellow, while the lower rim, which, though very sharp, is not nearly so salient, is of a pinkish brown colour. The internodes on a 5-foot stem are from 3 to 4½ inches in length. The culm sheaths are purple, with a pinkish tinge. The ligule and limbus very small, dressed with a few long purplish hairs on either side of the latter. They

have a few cross veinlets, which are for the most part replaced by dots. They soon wither and perish. The leaf
sheaths of the branchlets, which are borne in twos and threes,
are of a very pretty pink, and this, with the partly-coloured
stem and leaves, gives the plant an extremely ornamental and
peculiar tricoloured appearance. These sheaths are furnished
with long rather coarse purple hairs at the insertion of the
leaf. The bud scales are a very pale yellowish green.

The lanceolate leaves, in which the petiole is well marked,
are larger than in most of the Phyllostachys family. Some
of them are as much as from 8 to 9 inches long by nearly
2 inches broad, but they vary greatly. I have found as
many as eight secondary nerves on either side of the midrib. The tessellation is extremely neat and visible to the
naked eye. One edge is very sharply serrated, the other less
so. The colour is a glossy, rather dark green, beautifully
variegated with stripes, which at first are a bright orange,
fading presently to a creamy white. The lower face of the leaf
is glaucous, with the variegation rather sad-coloured and dingy.

One of my plants shows a curious deviation from the type
in the disposition of the colours. Some of the shoots have
self-coloured dark green leaves without any trace of variegation ; and where this is the case the colouring on the stems
is reversed, the groove of each internode being yellow and the
rest green—an elaborate freak of Nature which it requires more
learning than I possess to account for, or even to theorise upon.

The Japanese name KIMMEI-CHIKU, "the golden brilliant
Bamboo," is appropriate and significant.

At Leonardslee this Bamboo has grown to a height of 9
feet 8 inches with a circumference of $2\frac{1}{4}$ inches.

PHYLLOSTACHYS BAMBUSOIDES

MANY and various are the impostors that have laid claim to this title, ARUNDINARIA SIMONI especially being a pretender to this or any other name. From Japan under this designation I received YA-DAKÉ, the "Arrow Bamboo," which turned out to be nothing but MÉTAKÉ under another name; and for a long time PHYLLOSTACHYS VIRIDI-GLAUCESCENS was made to do duty for this species, even in Botanic Gardens. But at last the real Simon Pure has been brought over from Hong-Kong, and the cheats are all sent out of court discredited and put to shame.

In some essential features PHYLLOSTACHYS BAMBUSOIDES differs from all the members of the Phyllostachys group which have reached us. It has been described as a cæspitose plant, whereas a leading characteristic in all the others is the active rhizome. The branches, instead of being much longer than the internodes, are comparatively short, and whereas in the other Bamboos of the family the branches are so disposed that the shortest of the three (where, indeed, the third is not wanting altogether) is in the middle, in this case it is the longest of the three branches which occupies that position.

In its native home the culms are said to grow to a height of from 10 to 12 feet. With me in their second year they are 5 feet high, with a circumference of about 1 inch. The wood is hard and tough, the cavity of the internode very small—not more than one-sixteenth of an inch. The colour is green at first, ripening to yellow. The nodes are not very prominent, the upper rim especially being more flattened than is usual. The branch-bearing side of the culm is flattened rather than grooved, as in the case of the other Phyllostachides. The internodes are long in proportion to the length of the culm; I have measured them up to 8 inches in a 5-foot stem. The zigzagging, so characteristic of the group, is very strongly marked. The culm sheaths are purplish, soon withering as in other species. I can detect in them a few cross veinlets. The ligule is long and cut up, fringed with coarse hairs. The limbus narrow and bent back. The branches are borne in triplets, the longest, as I have already said, being in the middle. On an 8-inch internode the longest branch measures only about 9 inches. The leaves are of various sizes, the largest about 8 inches long by 1¼ inch wide. In shape they are lanceolate, pinched in near the top and ending in a fine point, attenuated at the base to a well-defined petiole. The tessellation is fine and regular. The secondary nerves on either side of the midrib from five to seven. The edges are serrated —very sharply on one side. The colour of the leaves is a bright and cheerful green above, glaucous on the lower face.

In this country we have but a short acquaintance with this species, for I doubt whether a living plant was ever seen in England until it was introduced into Kew two years ago; and, if Munro be right, there are considerable variations both in its inflorescence and foliage. However this may be, for horticultural purposes it promises to be a valuable acquisition, and having stood out last winter (1895), may be pronounced hardy. It has the merit, moreover, of being absolutely unlike any other Bamboo that is grown in our gardens.

PHYLLOSTACHYS MARLIACEA

ALTHOUGH there is no classical authority for numbering this handsome species among the Phyllostachys group, it is impossible to doubt that it must be referred to that genus. All those outward characteristics (apart from the flower and seed, of which we know nothing) which are found in PHYLLOSTACHYS MITIS, AUREA, NIGRA, VIRIDI-GLAUCESCENS, etc., are present here, and it would be strange indeed if it should prove to belong to any other tribe. Indeed it presents such a marked likeness to PHYLLOSTACHYS QUILIOI, that I do not think that any expert could tell them apart without examining the wrinkled base of the stem to which PHYLLO-STACHYS MARLIACEA owes its Japanese name, SHIBO-CHIKU, "the wrinkled Bamboo," and which makes it so useful for canes and umbrella sticks.

I have but one plant of it, for it is a rare Bamboo not easily obtainable, which in its third year grew to a height of 8 feet, and, in spite of the check of last winter, has slightly added to its stature and greatly to its bulk in 1895. The culm, when freed from its sheaths, is very beautiful in colour, shining like dark green enamel. The internodes at the base of the stem are very close together, being not more than $1\frac{1}{2}$ to 2 inches apart. The nodes are well defined.

The grooves caused by the pressure of the branches are very distinct. The branches are long and graceful, borne in twos and threes, in which latter case one falls off. One branch is much longer than the other. The sheaths in their young state are a pinkish brown, deeply spotted with dark purple, like the sheaths of PHYLLOSTACHYS QUILIOI. They are tessellated, and have a small ligule and limbus, the former furnished with rather coarse brown hairs. The leaves vary in size, some being as much as 4½ inches long by three-quarters of an inch or 1 inch wide, lanceolate, with a fairly long petiole. Both edges are serrated, the one more conspicuously so than the other. The colour is an intense green on the upper face, glaucous on the lower. There are from three to five secondary nerves on each side of the midrib. The scales of the tiny buds, which are the embryo branchlets, are tipped with a reddish purple colour.

The habit of the plant is elegant, beautiful both in form and colour. The culms, when in the second year the branchlets are fully developed and have all their foliage, bending over in graceful arches.

BAMBUSA MARLIACEA was introduced some years ago from Japan, and named after M. Latour-Marliac. It is perfectly hardy, and scarcely lost a leaf in the great frosts of February 1895. In our climate it does not show signs of running much at the roots, the culms up to the present all growing close together.

PHYLLOSTACHYS HETEROCYCLA

(1893). Eut the plants which were received from Japan had only vertical roots without a scrap of active rhizome, and this must be developed before any stem buds can be formed. I have every hope that next summer new shoots may make their appearance, and that we may be able to claim the plant as thoroughly established.

It appears to be likely to grow into a tall Bamboo of the stature of PHYLLOSTACHYS MITIS, and perhaps equally slow to make a start in a new home. The branches are borne in twos and threes (the third falling off), one much longer than the other. The internodes are grooved by the pressure of the branches. The leaves are small, from $2\frac{1}{2}$ to 4 inches long by half an inch wide. They are bright green on the upper surface, glaucous on the lower, minutely tessellated, serrated more on one edge than on the other. They are finely pointed, and the petiole is well defined. The secondary nerves on either side of the midrib are from three to four in number. My plants having made no new growth I have only seen the sheaths of the branchlets, which have a ligule rather large in proportion to their size, but hairless, with a very small limbus. As might be expected from their glaucous colour, the lower surfaces of the leaves have a very fine covering of silvery hairs. The upper surface is practically smooth.

I believe that the first living plants of this species introduced into England were those received here and at Kew from Japan in the winter of 1893, though it was shown at Paris at the great Exhibition of 1878, and named HETEROCYCLA by Carrière.

PHYLLOSTACHYS KUMASASA OR VIMINALIS

A SPECIES as pretty as it is unique in character. Munro says : "This is certainly unlike any Bamboo I have seen," and quotes Stendel, who calls it "species singularis" and "peculiaris certe formationis et vix dubie distinctum genus." Munro talks of having only seen the upper part of a culm 6 feet long, which points to a far taller plant than it is with me and at Kew, where it is a dwarf not more than from 18 inches to 2 feet high. A Japanese catalogue gives 3 feet as the height which it attains in its own country. Was Munro misinformed as to the length of the culm of which his specimen was a fragment?

The culm is green, channelled on the branching side, almost solid, the fistula being so minute as almost to escape observation, and very tough. The rather prominent nodes, which are of a darker green than the rather pale stem, are from 1 inch to nearly 2 inches apart, and the internodes are prettily zigzagged. The sheaths, which are richly fringed with hairs, are purple, fading at the top, which gives the undeveloped culm a rather strange, mottled appearance. The ligule is small and also fringed with silky hairs. The limbus is infinitesimal and very short-lived.

The branches are borne in threes and fours and are not

more than 1 inch or 1½ inch long, sometimes less, though in this short space they have two or even three nodes. They are enveloped in sheaths longer than themselves and of very peculiar structure, resembling a purple stem flanked by two tissue-like membranes each ending in a pointed growth of the same texture on either side of a true leaf, which takes the place of the limbus. The leaves at first sight appear to be clustered in threes or fours, but close examination shows that each leaf is borne singly either upon a branchlet or a sheath. A large-sized leaf will be about 3 inches long by nearly 1 inch in breadth, pointed at the top and broadly rounded at the base, ovate in shape, resembling the leaf-like branches or cladodes of Butcher's Broom (Ruscus), whence Siebold named the plant " BAMBUSA RUSCIFOLIA." The petiole is rather long. The down on the lower surface of the leaf is plainly visible to the naked eye. The tessellation is very close and minute. Both edges are very sharply serrated with prominent teeth. The secondary nerves are six or seven on either side of the midrib.

By giving the name KUMASACA to this Bamboo, Munro has given rise to some difficulty. Sasa (in composition after a vowel zasa) is a Japanese version of the two Chinese words hsiao chu (small Bamboo), and is the generic name given by the Japanese to the dwarf Bamboos. Kuma signifies an edge or border. The etymology of the word kumazasa (barbarously altered by Munro into kumasaca) would seem to point to the ARUNDINARIA VEITCHII, on account of its leaves withering at the edge in winter, and so having a distinct edge or border. It is certainly often used in that sense by natives. As I have already pointed out, KUMASASA

is the name given by Japanese gardeners to BAMBUSA
PALMATA, and to ARUNDINARIA VEITCHII, the latter being
distinguished as the lesser KUMASASA. It is also apparently
sometimes applied by Japanese botanists to BAMBUSA TESSEL-
LATA or RAGAMOWSKI, while our English botanists, following
Munro, give it to PHYLLOSTACHYS VIMINALIS, the native name
of which is BUNGOZASA, probably from the province of that
name in the southern island of Japan. There is thus utter
confusion, and a triangular duel between science, etymology,
and common use which is most bewildering, and so long as
this lasts it would seem wiser to leave the Japanese names
alone, contenting ourselves with the European nomenclature.
But when science does find it necessary to adopt words taken
from a foreign tongue with which she is unacquainted, she
will do well to avoid altering consonants, as Munro did when
he made *saca* out of *sasa*, or she may get herself into dire
trouble. Try it upon a few English monosyllables !

Munro's barbarism is the more regrettable in that Von
Siebold's name RUSCIFOLIA seems so very appropriate; the
other synonym, VIMINALIS, appears to me to be the reverse.
But KUMASASA is simply a filching of the native name of
another Bamboo, with a special meaning indicating a special
character which this species does not possess, and is therefore
the worst of all.

NATIVE OF THE UNITED STATES OF NORTH AMERICA

ARUNDINARIA MACROSPERMA

THE solitary species from the United States of North America.
This Bamboo appears to vary in height according to its geo-
graphical position. In the Southern States it grows to from
10 feet to 20 feet, or even 35 feet high, while in the north it
does not exceed 10 feet. It is the typical Arundinaria described
by Michaux. The stems are round (sometimes slightly flattened on one side at the point of b anching), slender, and much-
branched. The sheaths are purplish in colour, very persistent,
and fringed at the top with a few rather coarse hairs. The
leaves are about 7 inches long by 1½ inch broad, the
upper face smooth, the lower face downy, having the edges
slightly serrated—very partially on one side. The secondary
nerves vary from six to fourteen in number. The leaves
are rounded at the base and petiolated. The veins are tessellated. Interesting rather from the fact of its being the one
representative of the family on the vast continent of North
America than from any special beauty of its own. Some
botanists divide the taller and shorter varieties into two
species, but Munro treats them as identical. M. Marliac

sends out a Bamboo under the name of BAMBUSA NEUMANNI
(it is called HERMANNI in the Botanic Gardens at Brest), which
appears to be the same plant as ARUNDINARIA MACROSPERMA;
indeed, both M. Marliac and M. Blanchard, the Director of the
Brest Gardens, so regard it, although they do not know from
what country their Bamboo was originally received. The
shrubby form, ARUNDINARIA MACROSPERMA SUFFRUTICOSA or
TECTA is the variety grown at Kew and here. It is a very
active runner and demands plenty of space.

Mr. Bean in his description of the plant in the *Gardeners'
Chronicle* of 10th March 1894, says: "Mr. Nicholson tells
me that in the Southern United States he saw immense
quantities of it fringing the flat, muddy banks of rivers, and
forming almost impenetrable thickets. These thickets are
known as Cane Brakes, and in the old slave days of the
Southern States were of the greatest service to fugitive negroes
for shelter and concealment."

I have tried growing this Arundinaria in dense shade and
in the open sunlight. I have perhaps not had the plant long
enough to form a definite opinion as to the merits of the two
positions, but it certainly seems, so far, to thrive best in
shade. The growth is taller, the leaves larger, and altogether
the Bamboo has a better appearance.

"Carey mentions that this grass, which was once common
in Kentucky, has become now nearly extinct there," Munro
p. 16.

NATIVES OF THE HIMALAYAS

ARUNDINARIA FALCATA

THIS Bamboo is described by Munro as belonging to a group of four species (the others being ARUNDINARIA KHASIANA, ARUNDINARIA INTERMEDIA, and ARUNDINARIA HOOKERIANA, all of which, seeing the great altitudes at which they are found in the Himalayas ought to be tried in this country), in which the flower-bearing and leaf-bearing culms are distinct, which flower and seed every year, and, dying down under the snows of winter, throw up new shoots from the stools in the succeeding spring. The slender culms, with prominent nodes, grow to a height of from 6 to 10 feet; the internodes from 6 inches to 1 foot in length. The branches are very numerous. The culm sheaths are loosely tessellated, with the cross veins running diagonally. The ligule is rather long and fringed. The limbus narrow, varying in length from half an inch to 1½ inch. The leaves are brilliant in colour and rather glaucous, especially on the lower face. They are from 3 to 6 inches long, pointed, and tapering to a petiole at their base. The secondary nerves on either side of the midrib are from two to six or more. The edges are serrated, the teeth being more marked on one side than on the other. The leaf sheaths are

very downy, and prettily fringed with longer hairs at the insertion of the leaf. As in their native country, so here, the
culms die down every year in the winter; and since in our
climate the new shoots do not make their appearance until the
summer is well advanced, it follows that for some months of
the year the plant is but a poor withered thing, and that, in
spite of its undeniable beauty when at its best, it cannot be
recommended for general cultivation under the difficulties by
which it must be surrounded in all but the most favoured
spots of our country. It is to be noted that in the temperate
house the plant seems to change its nature. Safe from the
attacks of snow and frost, its culms do not die down but remain green and flourishing like those of its congeners. The
home of ARUNDINARIA FALCATA is in the north-western
Himalayas, where it has been found as high as 12,000 feet
above sea level.

In my remarks upon ARUNDINARIA FALCONERI I have
drawn attention to the confusion which has existed between
it and ARUNDINARIA FALCATA.

ARUNDINARIA FALCONERI or THAMNO-
CALAMUS FALCONERI

A TALL and singularly graceful Bamboo, growing to a goodly
height in favoured localities even in the British Isles. But
in the Midlands it is sadly dwarfed, rarely growing to a
height of more than 8 feet, and is cut down to the roots
every year by the winter's frosts. Indeed, in many places
it seems to dwindle away, year by year throwing up feebler
shoots, until it finally disappears. It is, however, so beautiful
where it does succeed, even in its less vigorous form, that
it is worth a trial in a sheltered nook. In the year 1895
I saw a lovely specimen in a Surrey garden, where, dying
down every winter, it makes a most graceful growth of about
8 feet in the early summer. When I saw it in the month
of September it was a perfect picture of elegance. The
tapering culms are very slender in proportion to their height,
and both stems and foliage are of a most brilliant green.
The internodes of the culms are thickly covered with a
white waxy bloom. The leaves are about 4 inches long,
narrow, thin, pointed, and petiolated, with striated venation
on the upper surface, and having, according to Munro, a few
inconspicuous transverse veins on the lower surface very
far apart, but I have not been able to detect these. The
edges are slightly serrated. The secondary ribs or nerves

on the lower side on either hand of the midrib are from two
to three in number. The leaf sheaths are smooth, as it were
cut short at the top, without any fringe, and having an
elongated ligule, slightly hairy on the back (Munro).

Habitat, N.-E. and N.-W. Himalayas. Altitude, 7000 to
9000 feet.

The confusion between ARUNDINARIA FALCATA and THAM-
NOCALAMUS FALCONERI has been very general. The majority of
the plants hitherto cultivated in this country as ARUNDINARIA
FALCATA have proved to be THAMNOCALAMUS FALCONERI. Mr.
Osborne, gardener to Mr. Smith-Barry, at Fota Island, Co.
Cork, informs me that the late General Munro identified the
specimens grown there under the former name as true THAM-
NOCALAMUS FALCONERI. The so-called ARUNDINARIA FALCATA
flowered in the gardens of the Luxembourg, in the South
of France, and at Algiers in 1876. Mr. Smith-Barry's plants
flowered and seeded at the same time ; it is, therefore,
probable that the mistake in nomenclature was universal,
and that all these plants were truly THAMNOCALAMUS FAL-
CONERI. Indeed, if Munro is right, and so far as I know
this has never been called in question, ARUNDINARIA FALCATA
is simply a perennial herb, flowering, fruiting, and dying
every year, and shooting again from the stool in the spring.
The French and Algerian plants are spoken of in quite
another category, as plants with which flowering, fruiting, and
death constitute a rare phenomenon. Messrs. Rivière themselves seem to have had personal experience of only one
of the two species, and I cannot but think that they have
fallen into the common error of confounding THAMNOCALAMUS
FALCONERI with ARUNDINARIA FALCATA. It may seem pre-

sumptuous to call in question any statement issuing from
so high an authority, but all the evidence seems to point
to a mistake.

As regards the hardiness of the species, Mr. Osborne
writes as follows: "The above-named Bamboo (THAMNOCALA-
MUS FALCONERI) throws up numerous canes here from 20 feet
to 25 feet. I have often wondered at the reports in gardening
papers in England of its sending up canes from 6 feet to
8 feet high, but, unfortunately, I have learned the reason
this season. We had an unprecedented sharp frost in
January last (1894) which killed the tops of all the THAMNO-
CALAMUS, with the result that instead of throwing up a few
monster canes to the height mentioned, they have thrown up
numerous small canes about 6 feet or 8 feet high around the
old stools. It must take several years of very mild winters
before they reach their usual strength. Many other Bamboos
were not the least injured, as far as I could judge." The
frost registered at Fota was 26° Fahrenheit below freezing
point. From this it is evident that the species is not
thoroughly to be depended upon even in the usually warm
climate of the west of Ireland. How it fared in Devonshire
and Cornwall, where there are, or were, many fine specimens,
I have not heard. Messrs. Watson and Bean consider the
BAMBUSA GRACILIS of the French cultivators to be identical
with THAMNOCALAMUS FALCONERI. I can detect no difference
between the two.

Mr. Bean did not find any plants of ARUNDINARIA FALCATA
in any of the gardens which he visited in south Cornwall in
1893. Of THAMNOCALAMUS FALCONERI he found magnificent
specimens.

ARUNDINARIA SPATHIFLORA or THAMNO-CALAMUS SPATHIFLORUS

This beautiful species from the north-western Himalayas, Sikkim, Bootan, and Nepal, where it is found at an altitude of from 7000 to 10,000 feet, bids fair when established to prove one of the most ornamental Bamboos. I was at one time led to think that the true plant had not hitherto been introduced into this country; but at last, in August 1895, I found it flourishing in full grace and beauty in a Surrey garden, and was assured by the owner that it had not suffered in any degree during the great trials of the pre-ceding winter. I have since then obtained specimens from Messrs. Veitch of Exeter. The tallest culms which I have seen are only from 6 to 8 feet high, but in their own country they grow to a height of some 20 feet. They are a pale yellowish or pinkish brown in colour, slender, fistulous, very smooth, and much-branched at the nodes, which are fairly prominent and conspicuous for a very distinct white ring at the base of each. The internodes in the immature specimens which I have seen are about 4 to 5 inches in length. The leaves are small, from 2 to 3 inches long by a quarter of an inch across, the petiole is well defined, the shape linear-lanceolate, ending in a fine point. The texture of the leaf is very thin and delicate ; there is no roughness, no prominent midrib, the serration on one edge only to be discovered by the aid of a lens. The secondary nerves are from three to five on each side of the midrib.

Nothing could exceed the beauty of the plant which I saw in Surrey. It was most striking, and at once arrested attention. It had all the grace and delicate distinction of ARUNDINARIA FALCATA, and what higher praise could be bestowed upon it ? I am given to understand that it is found as an undergrowth in the great coniferous forests of the north-western Himalayas. Like ARUNDINARIA NITIDA, therefore (which, by the by, it somewhat resembles), it will probably be wise to plant it in a shady position.

ARUNDINARIA RACEMOSA

A NATIVE of the Himalaya range, found near Darjeeling, in Sikkim, in Eastern Nepal, and in other places, at heights varying from 6000 to 12,000 feet.

It is a small Bamboo of low growth, according to Munro from 2 to 4 feet high, though other authorities give it as much as 15 feet,[1] the stature probably varying according to the altitude at which it grows. The culms are brownish in colour, and very thick in proportion to their height, being from half an inch to as much as 2 inches in diameter. The pale leaves, glaucous on the lower surface, are long and narrow, very finely serrated, lanceolate, round at the base, or often tapering into a short petiole (Munro); the point is long and setaceous (bristle-like). The midrib is flanked on either side by from three to five secondary nerves. The tessellation is conspicuous on both surfaces. The sheaths are striated, fringed and ligulate, hairy in a young state, smooth later, the ligule fringed.

Munro says: "This species has very rarely been found in flower; and when in foliage only it is extremely difficult to distinguish it from THAMNOCALAMUS SPATHIFLORUS. The best

[1] At Derreen in County Kerry it grows to a height of 9 feet 10 inches. The plants are five-year-old seedlings.

marks of distinction are the roughness of the stem below the nodes, the long points to the leaves, and the membrane at the top of the vagina and below the articulation of the petiole, which is only slightly hairy. The leaves have often long hairs below."

The only specimen which I possess of this Bamboo is not sufficiently mature to show its characteristics. I am informed that it is largely used in the high mountain ranges as fodder, besides being employed for the many uses to which natives apply the whole family. The great altitude at which the plant grows in its native home, and the tessellation of the leaves indicate a perfectly hardy Bamboo, and this has been proved at Kew during the winter of 1895, which does not seem to have injured it. Whether it will prove to be of any great distinction as an ornamental plant, or whether it is only valuable to the curious as an addition to their collections, is a fact which remains to be proved. Time will show.

ARUNDINARIA ARISTATA

To Lord Annesley, I believe, is to be assigned the credit of having been the first to introduce this species into our islands, and it is to his kindness that I am indebted for the specimen in my possession. Though still travel-sick, it seems to indicate a bright and ornamental Bamboo, and as it flourishes at a height of some 11,000 feet in the north-eastern Himalayan range, and has tessellated leaves, there is every reason to hope that it will prove a valuable and hardy addition to our gardens. The culms of my plant are about 5 feet high, of a purplish brown colour. The internodes about 4 inches long, but from so immature a plant it is not possible to judge accurately of the ultimate development of which it is capable. The nodes are fairly prominent, the stems much branched.

The leaves are of a bright green colour, slightly glaucous on the lower surface. They are long and narrow, about 4 inches in length by a quarter or three-eighths of an inch in breadth, tapering to a very fine point. The petiole is quite inconspicuous or absent, the leaf appearing to be sessile. The edges are very slightly serrated; indeed, the teeth are hardly perceptible. There are from three to five secondary nerves on either side of the midrib, which is well defined

and prominent.   The tessellation is very prettily marked.
The leaf sheaths are fringed with soft silky hairs, the ligule
being very inconspicuous.   The culm sheaths are hairy and
very slightly tessellated, the cross veins being rare, at great
distances apart, and rather diagonally inclined.

BAMBOOS THE NATIVE HOME OF WHICH IS UNCERTAIN

ARUNDINARIA NOBILIS

THIS Bamboo, of uncertain origin, has been grown in various places under the names of ARUNDINARIA FALCATA, THAMNO-CALAMUS FALCONERI, and ARUNDINARIA KHASIANA, indiffer-ently. That it differs from each and all of these is perfectly manifest. Moreover, as it is impossible to identify it with any of the hitherto described Indian Arundinarias, I am inclined to the belief that it has been imported, in circum-stances now long since forgotten, from China. In this theory I am supported by a letter from Mr. Rashleigh of Menabilly in Cornwall, in whose garden the plant has been cultivated for more than half a century, which I have his permission to quote, and in which he says :—

Your suggestion that my Bamboo may have come from North-Western China has revived my recollection, that about 1836-38 my father's friend, Mr. Henry Alexander, an East-Indian director, procured for him from China a large parcel of seeds, which came in charming little china pots or vases ; and it was about this time that much atten-tion was drawn to the parent of the present race of these plants of Bam-boos which, during about thirty years or more, grew on (a fine plant unchecked by winters) in that part of the garden here which is still called the Chinese garden. I feel sure, however, that this Bamboo came here through the East India Company's directory.

It will be remembered that between fifty and sixty years ago, the date of this importation, the East India Company had still practically a monopoly of trade with China, and it was their officials who carried on relations with that country until some years later, 1842, when the opium war took place. I look upon Mr. Rashleigh's letter, therefore, as strong corroborative evidence in favour of my supposition.

Regarding it then as a hitherto undescribed species, I have named this Bamboo ARUNDINARIA NOBILIS, from its great stature and imposing appearance. At Menabilly it is growing in clumps 24 feet high : my far younger specimens promise to grow with great luxuriance.

The culms are tall, round, slender, and straight, with a cavity large in proportion to the girth ; the internodes are about 7 inches apart. The nodes are not prominent, but very conspicuous from their purple-brown colour in contrast with a yellowish stem ; the lower rim of the knot is broadly marked with gray. The culm sheaths are much longer than the internodes, which they overlap ; they are rather rough in texture, and show a few cross veinlets ; the ligule is small and much divided at the top into a sort of fringe (though there are no hairs), and the recurved limbus is short, narrow, and very perishable. At each node are a great number of branchlets, giving the plant a verticillate appearance. The leaf sheaths, purple in colour, have a very small ligule ; there are no hairs at the insertion of the leaf. The leaves are linear-lanceolate, from 2 to 3 inches long by rather more than a quarter or nearly half an inch broad ; they taper to a point, and end at the base in a dark purple petiole. The serration of the edges is very slight indeed. The leaves are striate, having no cross veinlets, but a number of pellucid dots. There are from three to four secondary nerves on each side of the midrib. The surface of the leaf, which is very thin and papery, is a bright green with the purple hue of the petiole continued. along the edge, the line of colour being broad at first, and gradually narrowing till it fades away near the point. The lower face equally shows this purple edging, but is slightly more glaucous than the surface. The roots are cæspitous.

Although this Bamboo cannot be called entirely hardy, still it is more so than either ARUNDINARIA FALCATA or THAMNOCALAMUS FALCONERI, the only other two Bamboos with striated leaves which are grown in our gardens. In ordinary winters the culms do not die, though the leaves are shed, but on the contrary in the spring new branches are formed in great profusion. Eight degrees of frost have not sufficed to strip the leaves. But a prolonged winter of intense severity like that of 1895 kills the culms to the ground without, however, injuring the roots. In Cornwall the old leaves do not fall until the early summer, when the new ones are ready to come out. In the Midlands, then, we may regard ARUNDINARIA NOBILIS as a deciduous Bamboo, and to that extent hardy. Its gigantic stature, beauty of colouring, and elegance of form give it an ornamental value as to which there cannot be two opinions.

It is, of course, a difficult plant to obtain, for where it does exist it is muddled up under wrong names with species to which it does not belong. The expert must seek for it painfully, and when he does find it, probably it will be under the name of ARUNDINARIA FALCATA, or ARUNDINARIA KHASIANA. It was under the latter title that it came into my hands.

ARUNDINARIA ANCEPS

A LOVELY waif, picked up at the sale of a dead nurseryman's effects by Mr. Jordan, the superintendent of Regent's Park, who very wisely bought the whole stock. What was its birthplace, how it came here, must remain a mystery; for the only man who could tell the tale is dead, and his books destroyed or lost. However, it has fallen into good hands, where it will be well cared for, and will be a pleasure to thousands in one of the very best of our London gardens. I have carefully searched such descriptions as we possess of the Indian Arundinarias, and can make it tally with none, so I can only surmise that it may be one more treasure from the imperfectly ransacked Chinese Flora. Its nationality being uncertain, and the species showing no one conspicuous feature by which it may specially be recognised, and which would lead to the choice of a descriptive name,—though it is obviously as a whole perfectly distinct,—I have ventured to name it ANCEPS,[1] the "Doubtful" Arundinaria.

At a little distance the habit of this Bamboo is so like that of ARUNDINARIA NITIDA, that the two species might at first sight be taken for one another, but there are marked differences not difficult to detect: 1st, The stems of A.

---

[1] Sequor hunc Lucanus an Apulus anceps—
HOR. *Sat.* ii. 1. 34.

NITIDA are of a purple-black colour, whereas those of
A. ANCEPS, purple at first, ripen to a greenish yellow or brown ;
2nd, The leaf sheath in A. ANCEPS has a circular fringe of
short bristly white hairs at the insertion of the leaf : this
is a feature not found in A. NITIDA, whose leaf sheaths are
hairless ; 3rd, The petiole and edges of the leaves lack the
purple tint which is conspicuous in those of A. NITIDA.

The culms of ARUNDINARIA ANCEPS are tall, round, smooth,
very slender and rush-like; I have seen them as much as 7
feet high, and shall be surprised if they do not attain a far
greater development. The cavity in a 4-foot stem is very
small indeed, not more than half the diameter of the wall.
The nodes are fairly salient, the lower rim sharply defined,
the upper rim more rounded and protuberant ; the colour of
the node is purple. The branches are purple in colour, very
slender, with comparatively long internodes. In the leaf
sheaths the ligule is hardly to be detected, but the little halo
of hairs at the insertion of the leaves is very persistent and
distinct, and markedly different from all the Arundinarias of
anything like kindred habit, such as FALCATA, SPATHIFLORA,
NITIDA, NOBILIS, and FALCONERI.

The tender leaves—about 2 inches long by about a quarter
of an inch wide, more or less—are of a very brilliant green,
rather more glaucous on the lower face, linear-lanceolate,
ending in a sharp point, and attenuated to a rather short
petiole. The tessellation is very minute and perfect. There
are from two to three secondary nerves on either side of the
midrib. Such serration as exists, and it requires a lens to see
it, is more on one side than on the other.

BAMBUSA DISTICHA

THIS charming little Bamboo has hitherto been sent out by nurserymen under the name of BAMBUSA NANA, a title which belongs to a totally different and tender species described by Roxburgh. It has great beauty and most distinct characteristics, being quite unlike any other member of the family, and this alone would give it a claim to have a name all to itself without usurping one to which it has no right. I have therefore called it BAMBUSA DISTICHA, on account of the peculiar arrangement of the leaves, which are carried alternately in two vertical ranks all along the stem and branches.

The culm, which is about 2 feet high, is green, rarely clouded with purple, round, fistulous, and zigzagged; it is very slender. The internodes are markedly variable in length, indeed, capriciously so, for I have seen before me a stem, in which an internode all but 3 inches in length is followed by one three-quarters of an inch long, while that again is followed by one which measures over 2 inches, whereas in most Bamboos the internodes, short at the base, lengthen towards the centre of the culm in regular progression, and grow shorter again as gradually: the nodes, without being very prominent, are well defined. The sheaths are downy at

first, but this feature disappears as they wither; the tiny
ligule is furnished with small hairs, and the limbus is, as
might be expected, very small. The branches are borne
singly ; the leaves are a bright green on both sides, tessellated,
and serrated on both edges. They are very small, about 1¾
inch to 2¼ inches long by three-eighths to a quarter of an inch
wide. They have a very minute silvery down, quite imperceptible to the naked eye, on both surfaces, especially towards the
base. In shape they are lanceolated, ending in a very small
petiole. Each side of the midrib has two to three secondary
nerves. The distichous arrangement of the leaves is most
characteristic and singular.

Altogether BAMBUSA DISTICHA is a lovely and most
attractive little plant. It was rather roughly handled by the
last two winters, but never quite lost its leaves; with the
renewal of summer it sprang into beauty again, and, as the
roots are great wanderers, soon began to make a thick carpet
of brilliant greenery, full of character and individuality.
The origin of this Bamboo is doubtful. Mr Watson of Kew
says, "it is most like Chusquea tessellata of New Granada
(Munro) of any of the specimens in the Herbarium." It may
possibly be the same as the species which the Japanese call
OROSHIMA CHIKU, but I am without any evidence as to its
being indigenous in Japan.

CHAPTER VII

THERE is nothing finite in science—nothing finite in the arts and crafts which are her handmaids. Certainly nothing in gardening; for year by year, almost day by day, new treasures are discovered, or old ones reveal new secrets; more especially in the matter of hardihood do we meet with surprises. For how many lustres was the Aucuba cribbed, cabined, and confined as a tender plant in greenhouses, until some kindly but audacious hand set it free? and now it is to be found in every London square, smut-begrimed and filthy, but glorying and rejoicing in its filth. And so it has been with many plants once marked with a capital G in every catalogue, but now thriving gaily in a climate to which they have accustomed themselves without difficulty. Not five years ago one of the most famous of our gardeners, looking at my newly-imported starveling Bamboos, said with the sneering grunt of the unbeliever, "They'll all die." The laugh is on my side now, for the rickety babies have grown into stalwart young giants, full of lusty life, with the joy of many days ahead of them. And the best of it is, that the great and unexpected success which has attended the acclimatisation of those Bamboos which we already possess is but a herald of further triumphs. For as yet we have only touched the fringe of what we may hope to achieve in the decoration of our wilderness gardens with the grace of these Royal Grasses.

When we consider that in Asia and in South America alike there are Bamboos, known hitherto only from the dried specimens in herbaria, growing at incredible altitudes —that among the Andes, for instance, there is one species, CHUSQUEA ARISTATA, which has been found at an elevation equal to the height of Mont Blanc,—we must believe, nay, we know that there is many a Sleeping Beauty only waiting till some lover shall carry her off from her mountain fastness, to awake under the faint but kindly rays of an English sun.

It must, however, be remembered that altitudes in tropical climates by no means represent the same temperatures that they do in Europe. I am assured that in Madras and Ceylon snow does not fall below a height of 9000 feet above sea-level; that in Khasia it does not fall below 7000 feet, in Sikkim below 6000 feet, and that at a height of 5000 feet the vegetation of Tenasserim is subtropical. But when these facts are discounted, it is still certain that the Himalayas are full of treasures which we do not yet possess. In India, however, there are a Forestry department and Botanical Gardens, under the direction of men of science, and all the machinery for learned exploration, and shortly, it may be hoped, will appear Mr. Gamble's great monograph on Indian Bamboos, published under the auspices of the Government, which will throw a totally new light upon the subject. It is safe to prophesy, therefore, that all that is to be found in the Himalayas fitting our climate will before very long be available.

The exploration of the Andes is a less hopeful matter. They are rich in species with tessellated leaves, growing at heights of from 4000 to 15,000 feet above the sea-level, and assuredly they should be laid under contribution. The great difficulty will be, that in the absence of great botanical establishments, such as those of India, the burthen must more or less fall upon private shoulders.

Africa is, so far as we at present know, a less promising field for the collection of hardy Bamboos ; but it must be borne in mind that the chief authority to which we have to look is still General Munro's monograph, which appeared in 1866, when the Dark Continent was still a mysterious fable-land. It is probable that since the European powers have penetrated its most hidden recesses many botanical secrets, as rich and as hidden as the gold which has so recently been discovered, will be brought to light.

A short while ago I believed that we had already exhausted the resources of China and Japan. But since then we know that one species certainly, ARUNDINARIA NITIDA, and probably two others, A. ANCEPS and A. NOBILIS, must be referred to that source. Both the Chinese and Japanese are excellent gardeners and cultivators, trained by heredity in the art of improving and adapting wild plants to the needs of their civilisation. From time immemorial they have been engaged in ransacking their native forests and mountains for the enrichment of their pleasure grounds, and it seemed to me most unlikely that such sharp eyes should have passed by any species of conspicuous merit in a genus which in

their view is the type of all that is most graceful and most
poetical in garden form. Moreover, they are essentially
a practical people, to whom the commercial and utilitarian
value of the Bamboo calls aloud with the chink of dollars.
Our European collectors have for many years had free access
to their gardens, and have thus had before them living
catalogues of all the daintiest and loveliest species, with the
result shown by the enumeration which I have given in the
preceding pages. For these reasons I was inclined to think
that from those gardens we had not much more to hope for.
This has already proved to be wrong. The Flora of China
especially is one of the richest in the world; our botanists
are only now beginning to examine it by the light of
western science, and it is dangerous, therefore, to hazard any
very definite opinion in regard to its capabilities. One of
our greatest botanists writes to me: "The Flora of North-
Western China is essentially Himalayan, with a profusion of
distinct rhododendrons; why not, then, of hardy Bamboos?"

Is it certain, even, that all the species actually in
cultivation in Great Britain have come under the observation
of experts? The three species which I have named above
must have been here for years, yet such has been the confusion of names that no one suspected their existence until
a few months ago. A new enthusiasm, however, has sprung
up, and there is a perfect craze for hardy Bamboos, so
that it may be hoped that none will in future escape notice.
The infection, moreover, is spreading in the New World as
well as in the Old; hardly a week passes without some new
and unknown correspondent writing to give or ask for
information. This cannot fail to give a great impetus to

collecting; and it is with the view of calling the attention of
collectors in various parts of the world to the subject that I
have drawn up a list of those species which appear to be the
most likely to succeed in this country, and to which the
numerous expeditions sent out in search of Orchids and other
rare plants might, in passing, turn their minds with profit.

I am aware that my list errs greatly on the side of hope-
fulness; but a trial, at any rate, will do no harm, even though
some species should be sentenced to death, others to imprison-
ment in the temperate house; while every new plant
flourishing in freedom will be a fresh joy added to our
gardens,—in every sense a survival of the fittest. Many of
these, no doubt, may only find a congenial home in the
warmest nooks of our islands, but some there are which may
assuredly settle down comfortably, cheek by jowl, with their
Chinese and Japanese cousins in the ordinary English
climate.

I may be forgiven for once more dwelling upon the
tessellation of the leaf as some evidence of hardihood. For
this evidence I claim no more value than is afforded by the
simple fact that no Bamboo without this character has
proved thoroughly hardy in this country. There are,
no doubt, tropical Bamboos with tessellated venation which
we could not grow, and therefore the test is an incomplete
one. But when we find it combined with a natural habitat
of great altitude, subject to the influences of frost and snow,
in plants surrounded by a non-tropical and alpine vegetation,
we have such good warranty for the hardihood of the species
that we may with faith attempt to acclimatise it here.

I append an index taken by continents of those species

described by Munro, with some others the names of which have been kindly furnished to me by Sir Joseph Hooker, which I should be glad to see introduced with, doubtless, many others unknown and undescribed :—

ASIA

ARUNDINARIA WEIGHTIANA (Nees).—Tessellated leaves. Nilghiri Mountains.

A. LONGIRAMEA (Munro).—Tessellated leaves. Hong Kong.

A. FLORIBUNDA (Munro).—Tessellated leaves. Ceylon.

A. GRIFFITHIANA (Munro).—Tessellated leaves. Khasian Hills.

A. WALKERIANA (Munro).—Tessellated leaves. Adam's Peak, Ceylon.

A. DEBILIS (Thwaites).—Habitat 6000 feet to 8000 feet above sea. Ceylon.

A. INTERMEDIA (Munro).—Sikkim. 7000 feet to 8000 feet above sea.

A. HOOKERIANA (Munro).—Native name PRAONG (Hooker). Sikkim. 4000 feet to 6800 feet above sea.

A. PRAINI (Gamble).—3500 feet to 7800 feet above sea. Naga Hills, Upper Assam. Not described by Munro.

A. CALLOSA (Munro).—Tessellated leaves. "Prickly-jointed Bamboo." Native name USKONG (Hooker). 6000 feet above sea. Khasian Hills.

A. HIRSUTA (Munro).—Tessellated leaves. 6000 feet above sea. Khasian Hills. "Spinous stems" (Hooker).

A. MICROPHYLLA (Munro).—Tessellated leaves. 6000 feet to 10,000 feet above sea. N.E. Himalayas.

A. ROLLOANA (Gamble).—5000 feet to 7000 feet above sea. Naga Hills. Not described by Munro.

A. JAUNSARENSIS (Gamble).—7000 feet to 8000 feet above sea. N.W. Himalayas. Not described by Munro.

PHYLLOSTACHYS STAUNTONI (Munro). Tessellated leaves. China.

BAMBUSA NUTANS (Wallich).—5000 feet to 7000 feet above sea. Nepaul, Silhet, Khasia, Assam, Sikkim. Native name in Sikkim, "MAHLO."

B. GRIFFITHIANA (Munro).—Tessellated leaves. Only once found by Griffith in the extreme north of Burmah, associated with numerous tropical plants. Only inserted here on account of the tessellation. Probably not hardy.

B. CANTORI (Munro).—Tessellated leaves. China.

R. APUS (Schultes).—Tessellated leaves. Mount Salak, Java.

B. CORNUTA (Munro).—Tessellated leaves. Java. Native name, "TRING EMBON."

B. RITCHETI (Munro).—Tessellated leaves. Bombay, below the fall of the Kala Nuddi. Native name "CHOOMAREE."

R. MASTERSII (Munro).—Tessellated leaves, Assam, Dibrooghur. Native name, "BENTIBANS."

CEPHALOSTACHYUM CAPITATUM (Munro).—Tessellated leaves. 4000 feet to 5000 feet above sea. Khasia, Sikkim.

C. PALLIDUM (Munro).—India, Mishmee, Burmah, Patkaye. 5000 feet above sea. Native name, "BETEE BANS."

DINOCHLOA TJANKORREH (Buse).—Inconspicuous tessellation. Philippine Islands, and 4000 feet above sea in Java, Mount Salak.

AFRICA

ARUNDINARIA TESSELLATA (Munro).—Tessellated leaves. 500 feet to 6500 feet above sea. Mount Winterberg, Caffreland, Mount Katberg. Closely resembling the ARUNDINARIA MACROSPERMA of North America.

NASTUS BORBONICUS (Kunth).—Tessellated leaves. Alpine, 1000 feet to 3000 feet above sea. Island of Bourbon or Réunion.

CEPHALOSTACHYUM CHAPELIERI (Munro).—Tessellated leaves. Madagascar. A climbing stem.

SOUTH AMERICA

ARUNDINARIA RADIATA (Ruprecht).—Tessellated leaves. The forests of Brazil.

A. AMPLISSIMA (Nees).—Brazil. 4000 feet to 5000 feet above sea.

ARTHROSTYLIDIUM LONGIFOLIUM (Munro).—6000 feet above sea. Venezuela.

A. SCHOMBURGKI (Munro).—6000 feet above sea. Guiana. Native name, "CURATA." Lowest internodes 12 feet to 16 feet long.

CHUSQUEA ULIGINOSA (Philippi).—Tessellated leaves. Chili, Valparaiso.

C. ANDINA (Philippi).—Tessellated leaves. Andes, on the fringe of the perpetual snow.

C. CULEOU (Gay, " Flora Chili ").—Tessellated leaves. Chili.

C. TESSELLATA (Munro).—Conspicuously tessellated leaves. Andes of Bogota. ? = BAMBUSA DISTICHA.

C. ARISTATA (Munro).—Conspicuously tessellated leaves. 13,000 to 15,000 feet above sea in the Andes, Ecuador, Quito.

C. FENDLERI (Munro).—6000 feet to 12,000 feet above sea. Venezuela, Ecuador.

C. DOMBEYANA (Kunth).—6000 feet above sea.   Peru, New Grenada, Bogota, Tolima, Ecuador.

C. QUILA (Kunth).—Tessellated leaves.   Chili, Valparaiso, Valdivia, Chiloe.

C. SELLOVII (Ruprecht).—Tessellated leaves.   Brazil.

C. GAUDICHAUDII (Kunth).—Tessellated leaves.   Rio de Janeiro.

C. CAPITULIFLORA (Trinius).—Tessellated leaves.   Brazil, Rio de Janeiro.   Native name "QUIXIUME."

C. CAPITATA (Nees).—Tessellated leaves.   Brazil.

NASTUS BARBATUS (Ruprecht).—Tessellated leaves.   Mountain forests of Brazil.

GUADUA ANGUSTIFOLIA (Kunth).—Tessellated leaves.   2400 feet above sea.   Western slope of Andes, New Grenada, La Paila, Bogota, Ecuador, Peru.

G. AMPLEXIFOLIA (Presl).—Tessellated leaves.   2000 feet above sea.   Mexico, Santa Cruz, New Grenada, Venezuela.

CHAPTER VIII

THERE are some folk who object to the planting of Bamboos
in English pleasure grounds. They say that such manifestly
exotic plants give a foreign and unhomelike appearance to
the garden; that they are out of place, fantastic, and what
not besides! Are not the Briar Rose, the Holly, the Gorse,
the Hazel, and many others, far more beautiful than all the
plants which have been brought from abroad with infinite
pains and at great cost? No one denies the loveliness of the
Briar Rose and its companions, but even their charms can be
shown to greater advantage when set out with other and
still more brilliant plants, which, though not natives, are at
any rate willing refugees here. Rubies and diamonds are
not found in England, yet our English women are no less
fair for wearing them, and would be sorely troubled if
sumptuary laws were to be passed restricting them to the
use of British pearls. Our gardens, like our dames, challenge
the world for natural beauty. Their ornaments, from time
immemorial, they have drawn from over the seas. It is
right that we should take everything that is beautiful
wherever we may find it; it is certain that we shall hit
upon some spot in which it will blend harmoniously with

o

what already exists; and it is in the discovery of that fitting
place that we shall show our skill and our knowledge.   But
there has been so much heretical doctrine preached upon
this subject, that I would fain have my say in defence of my
Bamboos and other fair plants which have been so unjustly
vilipended, taking for my text Bacon's famous saying,
"God Almighty first planted a garden, and indeed it is the
purest of human pleasures."

Many years ago I was travelling with a companion in
Asia Minor, and we passed some days in the Troad.   It was
before the days of Schliemann's great discoveries, and we,
full of young ambition and presumption, thought that
perhaps for us the centuries might have guarded the secrets
of King Priam's treasure-house, and that to our lot might
fall the glory of fixing the site of the buried city.   In vain
we sought, thermometer in hand, for the warm springs at
which the deep-bosomed Trojan dames were wont to wash
peplum and chiton; in vain we tried to fix the positions of
the great gates, and dug in every mound for relics of the
mighty dead.   We were not possessed of the talisman
which should charm the guardian Afrits into revelation of
the mysteries committed to their charge, and we went away
no wiser than we came.   Had we but been armed with
King Solomon's seal we should have been famous, and
Schliemann an unknown nonentity.   Fate willed that it
should be the other way.

If, however, we did not find the city of Troy, we never-
theless were not without our Homeric experiences.   Well do
I remember how, on one occasion, the god descended into
the river Scamander, and there was a mighty flood, and we,

wet to the bone under torrents of rain, were separated from
our baggage for two days, and had to take refuge in a
Turkish farmhouse, where, during the hideous nights, we
fed the hungry myriads that formed the subject of the
famous riddle which drove Homer to despair and death.
Happily, however, memory makes light of mischances, and it
is the loveliness and delight of the days that followed which
remain crystallised in my mind—days when we wandered
through the Ida Range amid scenes so entrancing that one
understood how the burning imagination of the old Greek
poets peopled them with gods and goddesses, wood nymphs
and water nymphs, beings more ethereal and more beautiful
than the children of men, and yet capable of revealing
themselves to, and even of loving, and being loved by, those
few happy mortals to whom the supreme gift of the favour
of Olympus should have been vouchsafed.   I remember how,
during the lower part of the ascent of Mount Ida, we rode
through the enchanted forest and among the pastures where
young Paris tended his flock, and Aphrodite used to console
the solitudes of Father Anchises.   (How hard it is, by the
way, that Paris should seem always young, as young to-day
as when he went a-courting Helen ; while Anchises, who
charmed the Queen of all charms, is nothing but a blear-
eyed wreck, in order to bring into relief the everlastingly
priggish piety of pious Æneas!   a strange case of poetic
injustice!)   I remember how one longed to stop and dream
away the lovely noontide under the shade of the great trees
—Oaks and Chestnuts and Pines, and others whose names I
knew not; but it was enough for me that they were the
descendants of the very trees of Homer, as it was enough for

me to know that every tiny rill that whispered over the
great moss-grown stones, glimmering through a carpet of
daintiest wild flowers, would fight its way down to join the
rushing Scamander in the plain, just as it had done in the
days of the ten years' siege. It was my first taste of the
East. The sunshine was brighter, the shadows were darker
than any that I had seen before, and over dell and glade and
rockbound burn there was a glamour of sensuous beauty,
new, strange, and bewildering. Nor was there room to
doubt that Homer himself must have travelled through the
mountain forests that he described. For as we went
upward, the vegetation, so luxuriant below, became scantier
and scantier until it dwindled into mere scrub, and finally
ceased altogether ; then came a stiff climb across loose
shingle, where hardly a lichen was to be found, and over
which we had painfully to drag our unwilling horses until
we reached the summit. There, wonder of wonders! after
the long and weary tramp over barren rock, there burst
upon our view the very carpet of flowers which marked the
spot where the Lady Hera, having borrowed the girdle of the
Goddess of Love, decoyed the cloud-compelling Zeus.
Old Homer must have seen this strange sight, and invented
the pretty fable to account for it. He could not have been
born blind.

Ah! Mother Ida! many-fountained Ida! "your beauty
haunts me like a fever dream!" Crags and fells, groves
and streams, all are visions of supreme loveliness. It is the
gardening of the gods, inimitable, unapproachable, and yet
conveying a great lesson. Happily for the world, though
there are few scenes to match those which inspired the old

Greek poets, still there are not many countries where Nature has not dedicated some favoured school to teach man the same object lesson, if he would only profit by it. And yet there are still men whose ambition it seems to be that their Neptune shall throw up a spout of water a yard higher than somebody else's Triton, and who would fain, according to the measure of their means, ape the extravagant vulgarities of Versailles or Sydenham. They forget that these masses of stone abominations, though they may be triumphs of engineering skill, are no more gardening than are the fortifications of Vauban, and that the highest art being the concealment of art, that man is the greatest gardener who shall, on however humble a scale, have successfully imitated the master touch of Nature. In the garden of Eden there were no flower-beds, and the fairest and most bewitching scenes of this earth are those in which we can picture to ourselves Adam and Eve, before sin and carpet-bedding had been invented, wandering hand in hand, happy and contented with the mere sense of life and beauty and love, surrounded by the bountiful profusion of Nature, and soothed by the rushing music of sweet waters. Such a spot I can yet see in my mind's eye far away on an island of the Malay Archipelago,—a lovely vision of a crystal clear pool, fed by the glistening jewels of an overhanging cascade, sheltered from the heat of noon by a network of Palms and Bamboos, and strange vegetation draped with giant climbers. Birds, and butterflies as big as birds, of every dazzling colour of the rainbow, flit from bough to bough. The air is heavy with the scent of spices; Orchids and mysteriously-shaped flowers peep out as surprises amid the giant foliage; while great apes, chattering with uncontrollable fun, fight mimic battles with tropical fruits for ammunition, or gravely assist in one another's toilet.   Here again is the gardening of the gods—no formal beds, no torturing and trimming of Alternantheras, no setting out of geometrical patterns with House-leeks.   And yet what beauty of form! what incomparable harmony of colours!—a memory the light of which the changes and chances of thirty years have not been able to extinguish.

It is good to be able to record the fact that though there are still found prophets to bless the so-called architectural school of gardening, and even to write books advocating its adoption, the professors of these heresies find fewer acolytes year by year, while men more and more consult Nature as the true fountain-head of the gardener's craft.   As for those books and their writers, have they not been pilloried and annihilated, and utterly wiped out by the accomplished author of the *English Flower Garden,*—himself a true apostle of Nature, and a deadly foe to the intrusions of the stone-mason into the garden that he knows how to love. And yet I would guard myself against being misunderstood. There are, of course, many gardens where the natural configuration of the site has made a terrace, or even a succession of terraces, a matter of necessity, where, in fact, nothing could have been achieved without them.   There are many such where great beauty has been attained by the skilful combination of architecture with plant life.   Who can deny the merits and distinction of some of the famous Roman gardens, or of many of the Scotch and Welsh hillside pleasaunces?   What I am chiefly concerned to criticise are the acres of paving stones surrounded by balustrades, and bespattered by jets of greater or lesser size, which were dear to the French architects.   In these stones there is no beauty and but one sermon—" Vanity of vanities, saith the preacher, vanity of vanities ; all is vanity." Versailles is a wreck, and the rays of the Roi Soleil are extinguished for ever.

In these heavy masses of masonry there is only dignity for those who admire that which is costly.   The poetry of gardening lies in another direction.   Who can conceive a Dryad making her home in an Orange-tree incased in a green wooden tub ?   What nymph who respects herself would bathe her dainty limbs among the glorified squirts of Sydenham ? Another test : Could a painter paint these formal gardens of ashlar ?   Could a poet find inspiration in them ?   Would Saint Bernard say of them what he said of the woodland, " Aliquid amplius invenias in sylvis quam in libris " ?

He who would lay out for himself a paradise—I use the word in old Parkinson's[1] sense—cannot do better, having the needful leisure, than set out to drink in wisdom in Japan. Not in the Japanese gardens, for, as we shall see presently, nowhere is the gardener's work more out of tune with Nature than in that country of paradoxes ; but on the mountain side, in the dim recesses of the forest, by the banks of many a torrent, there the great silent Teacher has mapped out for our instruction plans and devices which are the living refutation of the heresies of stonemasonry.   There are spots among the Hakoné Mountains, not to mention many other places, of which the study of a lifetime could hardly exhaust the

---

[1] *Paradisi in sole Paradisus terrestris, etc.*   By John Parkinson, apothecary of London, 1629.

lessons.   One reason which makes Japan such a rich field for
observation is that perhaps in no other country will you find
so many types of vegetation within so small an area.   The
sombre gloom of the Cryptomerias, the stiff and stately Firs,
Pine-trees twisted and gnarled into every conceivable shape,
flowering trees and shrubs in countless varieties, combined
with the feathering grace of the Bamboo, and all arranged as
if the function of each plant were not only itself to look its
very best, but also to enhance and set off the beauty of its
neighbours—present a series of pictures difficult to realise.
Fancy a great glen all besnowed with the tender bloom of
Cherries and Peaches and Magnolias in spring, or blazing with
the flames of the Maples to warm the chill October, and in its
depths a great waterfall leaping from rock to rock for some
hundreds of feet!   Here and there the soft brown thatch of
some peasant's cottage, or the quaint eaves of a Buddhist
temple, jut out from the hillside, while far down below you
are the emerald green patches of paddyfield, with great white
cranes stalking about in solemn state.   In such a glen you
may sit hour after hour, feasting your eyes in wonder, and
learning how to get the fullest value out of your treasures at
home.   Few if any of the plants which you are admiring
are too tender to be grown in England, and the fair
landscape before you furnishes the key to their successful
adaptation.

The Japanese are true lovers of scenery ; no people have
a keener feeling for a beautiful landscape; to them a moon
rising over mount Fuji is a poem, and their pilgrimages to see
the almonds in blossom or the glories of the autumn tints
are almost proverbial—and yet, strange to say, in their gardens

they seem to take a delight in setting at defiance every one of
those canons which Nature has laid down so unmistakably
for those who will be at the pains to read them. The Japanese
garden is a mere toy that might be the appanage of a doll's
house. Everything is in miniature. There is a dwarf forest
of stunted Pines, with a Lilliputian waterfall running into a
tiny pond full of giant gold fish,—the only big things to be
seen. There is a semblance in earth and stones of the great
mount Fuji, and in one corner is a temple to Inari Sama, the
god who presides over farming, and is waited upon by the
foxes. Stone lanterns of grotesque shape spring up here and
there, and the paths are made of great flat stepping-stones
set well apart so as not to touch one another; shrubs, Cycads,
and dwarf Conifers are planted, not without quaint skill and
prettiness, but there are no broad effects, no inspiration of
Nature. It is all spick and span, intensely artificial, a miracle
of misplaced zeal and wasted labour. Attached to some of
what were the Daimios' palaces in the old days there were
some fine pleasure grounds, well laid out, rich in trees, and
daintily kept. The gardens of the Mikado, by the shore of
the bay of Yedo, are beautiful. But the average Japanese
garden is such as I have described it,—a mere whimsical
toy, the relic of an art imported from China, and stereo-
typed on the willow pattern plate.

In my little garden at Tokiyô—such a lovely spot over-
looking the bay!—there was a small pond in which myriads
of mosquitos used to live and love, bringing up innumerable
families, and making life almost intolerable. At last I could
bear it no longer, so I filled up the pond and made a sort of
bog garden of it, the chief feature of which consisted of great

clumps of Iris Kæmpferi. It was wrong, it was heterodox, it almost broke my gardener's heart. For if there are laws, sacred, immutable, as to the disposal of a few flowers in a vase, how much more is the laying out of a garden a matter not to be lightly tampered with! And yet when the iris came into bloom the following year, even the greatest sticklers for precedent among my Japanese friends were enraptured at the beauty of an innovation only pardonable in a barbarian.

The secret of the success lay in the massing of the plants —another lesson learnt from Nature, but nowhere better taught than in some of those lovely valleys of Mongolia which lie beyond the great wall of China. I was travelling in those regions in 1866. I knew nothing, but my comrade was a good botanist and ardent lover of flowers, and I can well remember how he kept jumping off his horse, as it seemed to me every few yards, to gather some precious rarity. We must have trampled treasures under foot which I, blind bat that I was, should have ridden past uncaring and un- thinking but for my friend. Yet, ignorant as I was, it was impossible even for me not to be struck by the picturesque and bold grouping of the flowers with which the valleys were enamelled. Nature had laid on her colours from a rich and generous palette. I can even now call to mind a great isolated crag some five or six hundred feet high, standing out from the mountain wall, on the summit of which, by efforts little short of miraculous, a small Buddhist temple had been made to perch. Every cranny and fissure of that great mass of rock seemed to be filled with lovely flowers and ferns, and at the base was a flame of scarlet Turk's-cap Lilies growing by scores against a background of some scrubby Pine or Juniper. That day I felt that I learnt how Nature intended Lilies to be planted; and that was how Tarquin grew them,[1] As I have said before, at that time my ignorance of plant life was complete; but I had a great leaning to all that is beautiful and picturesque, and so my travels in many lands were insensibly an education in gardening. It is true that it was the garden and not the flower that attracted me, but the joy that I took in the one led to the study of the other, and so the great love of both was built up.

To return to my Lilies. It is strange how the value to be obtained by planting great masses of one flower together is forgotten or neglected. How often, for instance, does one see stowed away in some corner a single plant of Erica carnea or Omphalodes verna, which ought to be grown by the hundred, or rather by the thousand! How rarely do you find the pretty little blue lobelia planted otherwise than in a thin, ineffective line! and how charming it is when you do come upon a great clump of it! I know a garden to the west of London where there is a really fine collection of plants, especially of herbaceous plants. They are grown with loving care; they are all planted in soil scientifically prepared to suit their several natures, and scrupulously labelled, so that every plant stands out with its rank and titles ostentatiously set forth in English and in Latin. No new rarity is announced in the nurserymen's catalogues but what it at once finds its way into

---

[1] Hortus odoratis suberat cultissimus herbis,
   Sectus humum rivo lene sonantis aquæ.
   Illic Tarquinius mandata latentia nati
   Accipit, et virga lilia summa metit.
                                   OVID, Fasti ii. 703.

those all-absorbing borders, of which there are hundreds upon
hundreds of yards. All the treasures of the uttermost ends
of the earth seem to be gathered together there; but none is
allowed to gladden the eye by showing off its true beauty.
Background there is none ; and if there be six, or sixty, or any
number of one species, they are all dotted about singly,
separated from their fellows, and compelled to consort with
any uncongenial stranger that chance or the gardener's trowel
may have established by their side. In winter, when the
leaves have died down, the labels in the long dreary borders
look like a procession of Lilliputian tombstones—a very
necropolis of plants. Here are love, money, and labour
lavishly expended, and all lost for want of a little attention to
that teaching which Nature so unmistakably gives us. If a
man is making a pleasaunce for himself, then, as it appears to
me, beauty is the first object, and this in any garden may best
be obtained by having a few varieties liberally displayed in
such a framework of other plants as will set them off to the
best advantage. If a botanical collection be the aim in view
that is another matter; but then the plants should be set out
according to families and in purely scientific array. That is
a great and a laudable object. But to turn what should be
a garden of delight into a mere living illustration of the
advertising lists—to look upon rarity and crackjaw names as
the highest goal of the gardener's ambition, that is a view
with which I for one have no sympathy. And yet it is a
vice of which there are many amateurs. Fiends there are
who haunt flower shows, and are assiduous attendants at
lectures, bores from whom there is no escape—mostly feminine,
but some apparently neuter—flinging painfully-acquired

sesquipedalian names at their victim's heads with an air of
conscious superiority. It is strange that one never hears of
those plants a second time. I believe that if they ever
existed they die of despair, killed by their names!

When all is said and done, it is certain that though there
are many bad and ugly gardens in England, still there is no
country in the world that can show so many really beautiful
pleasure grounds, and that the number of these is increasing
as taste improves and larger views prevail. Washington
Irving is not the only traveller who has done homage to our
skill as landscape gardeners. There are many reasons which
combine to give England the pre-eminence in this respect. In
the first place, there is the much abused climate. Foreigners
may sneer as they please at our fogs and our gray skies,
but with all their contempt where can they show such turf
and such trees? and are not these the foundation of all
gardening? It was a wise as well as a gallant Frenchman
who asserted that the most beautiful thing in nature is an
English girl, mounted on an English horse, on English turf,
and under an English tree. True it is that the rays of the sun
caress rather than scorch up our plants; but our vegetation
is the greener, and our flowers last the longer, not meeting
the fate of Semele. After all there is some malice and not
a little envy in the attacks upon us. If I were asked to quote
the most insolent speech that ever was made in polite society,
I think I should cite the reply of the Neapolitan ambassador
(to Sir Robert Walpole, I think), when he was asked to admire an effect of sunlight on the Thames at Chelsea, "La
lune du Roi mon maître vaut bien votre soleil." After all
we may be contented with a climate that admittedly gives us

beautiful women, beautiful horses, beautiful turf, and beautiful trees.   But that is not all; it is certain that, in spite of fickle weather, we can and do cultivate more varieties of plants than can be seen in any other country.   What quarter of the globe is there that has not been laid under contribution to enrich and beautify our gardens ?   There are many English pleasaunces which are in themselves a liberal education in geography.   Here are Pines from California, China, Mexico, Sardinia ; Fir-trees from the Black Sea and Colorado ; great Flame Flowers, Tritomas, from the Cape of Good Hope; a carpet of Acæna from New Zealand ; Tulips and other bulbs from Asia Minor; herbaceous plants from Central Asia ; Bamboos from China and Japan and the Himalayas ; the Chusan Palm ; the Edelweiss of the Alps; the Honeysuckle of the Pyrenees ; and every recurring season tests the resisting power of some new plant.   It is a never ceasing wonder that all these, and thousands of others, all different in nature and in origin, can find a congenial home in this Protean climate.   Perhaps it is the very fact of the variations in our weather that gives us this boundless and varied wealth to choose from.

Then there is the extraordinary power inborn in the Englishman of making a home for himself wherever he may be.   Not only does he travel more than other people, but wherever his fortunes lead him—whether as colonist, soldier, or diplomatist—there he at once sets about establishing himself as if the remainder of his life were to be spent there, and his ambition is to " settle,"—a word untranslatable in any other tongue, because the idea is absent.   In a French colony there is no such thing as the " settler,"—the man who comes prepared to stay if needs must, and perhaps even found a family.   The

Frenchman, differing in this from us, dreams only of the day
when he shall return to his beloved café on the Boulevards,
and in the meantime is content to sip his absinthe in as good
an imitation of that same café as circumstances will admit.
The Spaniard, the Italian, the German are better colonists
than the Frenchman, but the idea of making a home, even for
a short time, is peculiar to the Englishman ; and of his home
the garden is an essential feature. In many lands are such
gardens found, and they exercise an influence over much of
the work that is done in this country. There are hundreds
of gardens in England which have some feature inspired by
the memory of the owner's little patch of pleasure ground
thousands of miles beyond the seas; others there are that,
furnished with seeds of plants from some banished friend,
reflect the descriptions given in his letters. But even when
men have simply travelled much, keeping their eyes open to
see what is beautiful, without of necessity remaining for any
length of time in one place, they come back with new ideas
insensibly acquired, pictures indelibly fixed in their minds,
which they cannot but strive in some measure to reproduce
when the chance occurs. And so it is that in English gardens
and pleasaunces there is so often a memory of many lands
enshrined amid the charms of our own scenery.

As in all arts, so in gardening, there is a school which
prides itself upon having purer methods than those which are
followed by the general. To these purists it is a sin that we
should introduce foreign trees into our pleasaunces. "England
for the English" is their motto, and they resent the intrusion of
any foreigner among their Elms, and Oaks, and Ashes, and
Chestnuts. But then they should be consistent. It suits them

to forget that those very Elms and Chestnuts which they look
upon as the legitimate ornament and pride of their landscape
are themselves aliens, the one an Italian, the other an Asiatic.
" Time," say the objectors, " has washed them from the stain of
birth and given them the rights of citizenship ; " time will perform the same kindly office for many another beautiful plant.
Sadly, indeed, would our plantations be shorn of their glories
if all evergreens save those which are indigenous were to be
banished from them, and we were restricted to the natives
which you may count on the fingers of your two hands. No !
our gardens, like our race and our language, owe their merits
to the continual infusion of new blood. Indeed, it would seem
as though race and language were in far greater danger from
intruders than our Flora, for every steamer that reaches our
ports discharges a load of indigent aliens, while even in the
days when Dryden was king over the wits of the coffee-houses,
he complained that " if so many foreign words are poured in
upon us, it looks as if they were designed not to assist the
natives, but to conquer them."

In rightly using, then, the great gifts which we have
received from beyond the seas, we should, to borrow Dryden's
phrase, " assist the natives," not " conquer them." For there
are undeniably certain characteristics peculiar to the English
landscape with which it would be treason to interfere. As I
write, I look out upon a great rolling tract of park land
studded with patriarchal Oaks that were saplings in Planta-
genet and Tudor days, giant Ash-trees, Elms, and Thorns
planted in the reign of good Queen Anne. Far be it from me
to introduce any change in such a scene. It is thoroughly
English and perfect of its kind ; no impious hand should dare

to tamper with it. But farther up the hill there is a spot
snugly screened from the cruel blasts which come from north
and east, where, when the great oaks and elms, shorn of their
summer bravery, are mere gaunt skeletons, there is still
some shelter and some warmth. Here, amid the sparkling
glitter of a holly grove, are all manner of beautiful evergreens
—rare pines, steepling fir-trees, rhododendrons, cypresses,
junipers. A tiny rill trickles over the green velvet of the
rocks, with ferns peeping out of crannies in which many an
Alpine treasure is hushed to rest, waiting the warm kiss of
spring and the song of the birds, that, like Orpheus with his
lute, shall raise the seeming dead from the grave. Tall rushes
and gracefully arching Bamboos, hardly stirred by the wind,
nod their plumes over the little stream from which the rays
of a December sun have just strength enough to charm the
diamonds and rubies and sapphires; a golden pheasant, all
unconscious of a human presence, is preening his radiant
feathers by the water side. It is a retreat such as the fairies
might haunt, and where in the bitter Christmastide a man
may forget the outside world, and for one too brief hour revel
in a Mid-winter Day's Dream of glorious summer. In the
planning of this sun-trap surely the most captious critic will
not cavil at the addition of such strangers as may seem best
suited to fill in a scene which may not be English, and yet is
in harmony with, and lends a new charm to, the surroundings
with which it is contrasted.

Whatever may be the cause—and now that one may put a
girdle round the earth in little more time than it took to ride
post from the Land's End to John o' Groat's and back a
hundred years ago, it seems evident that travel has much to

P

say to it—the improvement in our gardens is most conspicuous. And in truth we have unlearnt as much as we have learnt. To own an historic house and gardens, like Levens, for instance, which have been undisturbed and unchanged by the revolutions of centuries, is a matter of which a man may well be proud. Nor is it only the interest of antiquity which attaches to such relics of a bygone age, for there is a certain impressive beauty in their stateliness which cannot be denied. Yet would it be unwise to plant in that way to-day. The stamp of nobility which time alone can give would be wanting. Yew or box trees fantastically carved and tortured into all manner of whimsical shapes cannot be achieved but by patience and long years of waiting. Better results may be obtained with much less labour and greater rapidity, and the *ars Topiaria* is happily dead. Not so the hedge of holly or yew, which is a grave, dignified, and even necessary feature in many gardens, modern as well as ancient. Indeed, I have in my mind such a screen planted some thirty years since, sheltering a long row of beehives in a beautiful Scotch flower garden, the effect of which is most charming; but the birds and men, and beasts and ships and teapots, and the many other conceits of the pleacher,—nay, the very pleacher himself,—are as extinct as the dodo or the great auk.

Then there was a moment when the folly of fashion spent itself in the construction of abominations in the shape of grottos—probably inspired by the grand tour and the study of Virgil ; when every man, who had completed his education by a journey in Italy, or if he could not afford that expensive luxury, by reading a friend's letters from Naples or Syracuse, must needs contrive in his garden a den, the walls of which he lined with shiny pebbles, shells, bits of glass, and every incongruous rubbish that he could gather together. Among the most famous of these were Pope's grotto at Twickenham, "composed of marble, spars, gems, ores, and minerals," and that of the Duke of Newcastle at Oatlands Park, which was afterwards the residence of the Duke of York. Dr. Johnson's account of the former in his *Lives of the Poets* is too good not to be transcribed :—

> Here he planted the vines and the quincunx which his verses mention; and being under the necessity of making a subterraneous passage to a garden on the other side of the road, he adorned it with fossil bodies, and dignified it with the title of a grotto,—a place of silence and retreat, from which he endeavoured to persuade his friends and himself that cares and passions could be excluded. A grotto is not often the wish or pleasure of an Englishman, who has more frequent need to solicit than exclude the sun; but Pope's excavation was requisite as an entrance to his garden, and as some men try to be proud of their defects, he extracted an ornament from an inconvenience, and vanity produced a grotto where necessity enforced a passage.

After all, therefore, there was some excuse for Pope's folly, but what can be said for that of the Duke of Newcastle, over which the County history gloats with honest pride ?—

> The pleasure grounds are beautifully laid out; and a delightful walk through the shrubbery leads to a romantic grotto, which was constructed at a great expense for the Duke of Newcastle by three persons (a father and his two sons), who are reported to have been employed in the work several years. It consists of four or five apartments, the sides and roofs of which are incrusted with satin spar, sparkling ores, shells, crystals, and stalactites ; some of the quartz-crystals are unusually large and fine. There is also a bath-room, in which is a beautiful (marble) copy of the Venus di Medici, as though going to bathe. The rocks forming the exterior are built up with a whitish-coloured perforated stone, a kind of tufa. In the upper chamber the late Duchess of York passed much of her time when the Duke was in Flanders during the revolutionary war with France.

Like a cavernous Madame Malbrook! Grottos have gone
out of fashion now ; as Dr. Johnson pointed out, they did not
suit the climate; and then they were so manifestly incomplete : what is a spelunca without a great clumsy Polyphemus
ogling his Galatea with his one saucer-eye ?

Of carpet gardening—a disgrace which has sat heavily upon
us these many years—there is no need to say much; it
avails not to flog a dead horse, and this, if not dead, is at any
rate dying; as Bacon said of the fashion consequent upon it, of
tricking out patterns in coloured earths, sands, or pebbles,
" You may see as good sights, many times, in tarts."

The truth is that in every good garden there is a poetical
or spiritual beauty with which these crude and flaunting
artifices are out of tune; the air which breathed o'er Eden still
in some mystic sense pervades our groves. " God planted the
first garden ;" and if man was formed in His image, may we
not believe that certain more favoured spots still reflect the
idea of that first Divine Garden ? To catch the spirit of these
is the supreme art of the gardener, and leads him to the
realisation of the next proposition of the text, " the purest of
human pleasures."

I look upon gardening as one of the fine arts, and, rightly
understood, not one of the least difficult. The painter or the
sculptor makes his effects at once, and obliterates, or models
and remodels, until he has attained that at which he is
aiming. But the gardener has to consider not what his work
is now, but what it will grow into ten, twenty, fifty years
hence. He has to take into account not the present aspect
of his materials, but what are their capabilities in the future
and their relative powers of development. If he has a

background ready made to his hand he is lucky, but if he has
to make it he has to do so with trees which are mostly far
slower of growth than the more immediately effective plants
which it is their office to set off.   He has to balance questions
of soil, light, moisture.   All this involves not only the poetic
sense, but also great and patiently-acquired knowledge.   He
has no Aladdin's lamp wherewith to bid trees spring from the
earth and form a sheltering background, yet background is
the soul of all gardening, rarely, alas ! seen at its best by him
who has devised it.   If the background be unfitting all the
work is thrown away.   Colour, form, light and shade,
grouping, all have to be studied in the composition of one of
those living pictures which the gardener paints with living
materials.

In these days his choice of subjects is varied indeed, for
there is scarcely a portion of the globe from which he cannot
borrow some landscape with the aid of the wealth of plants
that the last half century has given us.   Are all these chances
and opportunities to be thrown away ?   Are the lessons that
have been learnt to be a vain thing ?   It seems to me to be
rank folly that we should fetter ourselves by rejecting all the
beauties of form as being incongruous, when no one dreams of
excluding those of colour.   No one ever repudiates a beautiful
flower because it is an exotic ; it is inconsistent, then, to refuse
admission to a lovely tree.   In nature it is to form, far more
than to colour, that the fairest pictures owe their charm.   You
may have to hunt for a flower, but the grace of a Palm or a
Bamboo springs into notice of itself.

So far as our present knowledge goes, with the single
exception of Fortune's Chamærops, the hardy Bamboos are the

only plants which help us to give, in certain appropriate places, some faint idea of the mysterious vegetation of warm climates. Outlanders it must be confessed that they are, with the impress of their foreign origin stamped on every feature, differing in that from many an impostor, too often undetected, that raises its bragging head with as much effrontery as if it could trace an English pedigree back beyond the Crusades. The impostor is admitted without a word, but give a place to the more honest and charming outlander, and you are a Goth, a destroyer of the English landscape when, turning an alley, you bring the purist to some secluded spot framing a picture which he cannot understand, and in his superiority will not admire, but which to you brings back something like a subtle fragrance of the dim far-away.

APPENDIX

NOTE ON JAPANESE NOMENCLATURE

As Japan must, for obvious reasons, during some years to come, be the principal source of supply of hardy Bamboos, it will be useful to collectors, and especially to nursery gardeners who are beginning to import these plants in large quantities, to have before them a list of such Japanese names as have, up to the present, been identified with their scientific or European equivalents. The list is manifestly and necessarily imperfect, but it is at any rate a first contribution on the subject, which future knowledge will supplement and perhaps rectify, though I believe that, so far as it goes, it is accurate. Where any doubt exists I have indicated it by a mark of interrogation.

BUNGOZASA, syn. GOMAIZASA = PHYLLOSTACHYS KUMASACA (Munro),
BAMBUSA VIMINALIS (French gardens),
B. RUSCIFOLIA (Siebold).

G. MADAKÊ, syn. KURODAKÊ, q.v.

HA-CHIKU = PHYLLOSTACHYS HENONIS.

HÔRAI-CHIKU, syn. TAIBÔ-CHIKU = PHYLLOSTACHYS AUREA.

HOTEI-CHIKU sent out as BAMBUSA STERILIS by Japanese gardeners, apparently the same as PHYLLOSTACHYS AUREA.

KAN-CHIKU = BAMBUSA MARMOREA.

KANZAN-CHIKU   = ARUNDINARIA HINDSII (Munro), BAM-
                                 BUSA ERECTA (French gardens).

KIKO-CHIKU, syn. KIMON-CHIKU   = PHYLLOSTACHYS HETEROCYCLA, BAM-
                                 BUSA HETEROCYCLA (Carrière). (The
                                 tortoise-shell Bamboo).

KIMMEI-CHIKU   = BAMBUSA (PHYLLOSTACHYS) CASTILLONIS
                                 (French gardens).

KIMON-CHIKU, syn. KIKO-CHIKU, q. v.

KOKUMAZASA   = ARUNDINARIA VEITCHII.

KUMAZASA   = BAMBUSA PALMATA, sometimes also
                                 ARUNDINARIA VEITCHII, for which,
                                 however, KOKUMAZASA or "the lesser
                                 KUMAZASA" is the more appropriate title.

KURODAKÉ, syn. GOMADAKÉ, KURO-CHIKU = PHYLLOSTACHYS NIGRA.

MADAKÉ   = (?) PHYLLOSTACHYS SULPHUREA (French
                                 gardens).

MÉTAKÉ or MÉDAKÉ   = ARUNDINARIA JAPONICA (Siebold).

MÔSÔ-CHIKU or MOUSO-CHIKU   = PHYLLOSTACHYS MITIS, PHYLLOSTACHYS
                                 EDULIS.

NARIHIRADAKÉ   = ARUNDINARIA SIMONI (Carrière).

OROSHIMA-CHIKU   (?) = BAMBUSA DISTICHA.

SHIBO-CHIKU, syn. SHIWA-CHIKU = PHYLLOSTACHYS MARLIACEA (French
                                 gardens).

SHIHO-CHIKU ⎫   = BAMBUSA QUADRANGULARIS.
SHIKAKU-DAKÉ ⎭

SUO-CHIKU   = BAMBUSA ALPHONSE KARRI, a variegated
                                 form (pink and green) of BAMBUSA
                                 NANA (Roxburgh), not hardy in this
                                 country.

SUDZU-DAKÉ   = BAMBUSA SENANENSIS (differing from the
                                 other species also called B. SENANENSIS,
                                 which is YAKIBAZASA = Arundinaria
                                 Veitchii), not known at present in this
                                 country.

TAIBÔ-CHIKU   = HORAI-CHIKU, q. v.

TAIHO-CHIKU   = BAMBUSA VITTATA ARGENTEA (French
                                 gardens), a silver variegated variety
                                 of BAMBUSA NANA (Roxburgh), not
                                 hardy in this country.

TAIMIN-CHIKU   = ARUNDINARIA HINDSII, var. GRAMINEA
                                 (Kew), BAMBUSA GRAMINEA (French
                                 gardens).

TAISAN-CHIKU	a tropical Bamboo (? B. VULGARIS) acclimatised in the hotter parts of Japan where it only puts forth shoots in late summer. Not hardy in this country.
YADAKÉ	= PHYLLOSTACHYS BAMBUSOIDES. (*N.B.*— Plants received from Japanese nurseries have not proved true to name.)
YAKIBA-ZASA (see also SUDZU-) DAKÉ	= BAMBUSA SENANENSIS, not to be distinguished from ARUNDINARIA VEITCHII

In time, when more consignments shall have-been received from Japan, it will be easy to identify all the Japanese names with their European equivalents. The difficulty of doing so at present lies in the fact that formerly when plants were received their Japanese labels were lost or destroyed as valueless by European nurserymen who, of course, were unable to decipher them; so the Bamboos were sent out under improvised and often inappropriate names, unless indeed they had the good fortune to be named by a skilled botanist, when some fitness of nomenclature was observed. Another stumbling-block has been the great number of provincial and even local names in Japan itself, while a third crux has been created by the native nurserymen, who have not always been over-scrupulous in sending out plants true to name. Perhaps, however, it is hardly to be wondered at that in a family where the distinctions are often exceedingly minute and inconspicuous, there should be almost the same confusion among nursery gardeners in the East as in the West. The great impetus which has been given to the cultivation of Bamboos in Europe during the last few years will, it may be hoped, be an encouragement to greater accuracy among the Japanese growers in future.

It must be borne in mind that TAKÉ (in composition,

after a vowel sound, DAKÉ) is a pure Japanese word signifying Bamboo. CHIKU is a Japanese corruption of the Chinese word CHU, Bamboo. The former of these is applied only to the tall or arboreous Bamboos. The latter is generic and is used for dwarfs and giants alike. SASA, in composition ZASA, is a Japanese corruption of the two Chinese words HSIAO CHU, signifying small Bamboo, and is only applied to the dwarf species of Professor Sargent's "forest floor." I have alluded to this before, but it may be convenient to repeat it here.

INDEX

BY THE SAME AUTHOR.

TALES OF OLD JAPAN. By A. B. MITFORD, Second Secretary to the British Legation in Japan. With illustrations drawn and cut on wood by Japanese artists. Crown 8vo. 3s. 6d.

ATHENÆUM.—"The reader will find much pleasant reading, which may be studied with advantage by all who are seeking for instruction about the country, or who are likely to have any relations with the natives. The selection which Mr. Mitford has presented to us carries us through the different aspects of Japanese life from the cradle to the grave."

ILLUSTRATED LONDON NEWS.—"A work of unusual interest and unexceptionable authority."

PALL MALL GAZETTE.—"These very original volumes have all the value their author claims for them and more. . . . They present us with pictures of Japanese life and manners not worked out in the monotony of minute detail, but dashed in with bold, telling touches. . . . They will always be interesting as memorials of a most exceptional society, while, regarded simply as tales, they are sparkling, sensational, and dramatic, and the originality of their ideas and the quaintness of their language give them a most captivating piquancy. The illustrations are extremely interesting, and for the curious in such matters have a special and particular value."

STANDARD.—"Mr. Mitford has collected both sermons and stories from authentic sources, and done his work as a translator with great freshness, vigour, and clearness of style."

SATURDAY REVIEW.—"Will be highly interesting to all. . . He has successfully rendered the Japanese idioms into pleasant and readable English, and has added much to the interest of his work by the illustrative commentary he has been able to supply on the manners and customs of the people gathered from his own experiences in the Land of the Rising Sun."

MACMILLAN AND CO., LTD., LONDON.

BY ALFRED AUSTIN,

POET LAUREATE.

THE GARDEN THAT I LOVE. With Illustrations. Sixth Thousand. Extra crown 8vo. 9s.

TIMES.—"It is a description in lucid and graceful prose of an old-fashioned garden and its cultivation, interspersed with genial colloquies between its owners and their guests, and enriched with occasional verse. Mr. Austin, who is greatly to be envied the possession of this delightful garden, and not less to be congratulated on his sympathetic appreciation of its charms, has rarely been so happily inspired. . . . Some of his admirers will wish for more of Mr. Austin's verse; for ourselves we are content with a volume which, though not in verse, is unmistakably the work of a poet."

SPECTATOR.—"We are glad to welcome Mr. Alfred Austin's delightful *Garden That I Love* in a compact book form. Mr. Austin is the laureate of gardens; he is, as Addison says, 'in love with a country life, where Nature appears in the greatest perfection, and furnishes out all those scenes that are most apt to delight the imagination.' *The Garden That I Love* is sure of a large and appreciative audience."

IN VERONICA'S GARDEN. With Illustrations. Fourth Thousand. Extra crown 8vo. 9s.

SPEAKER.—"The charm of his subject lies upon the book, so that even the list of flower-names becomes fragrant."

TIMES.—"Mr. Austin blends in very delightful fashion his love of flowers and of simple rural delights with his love of gentle thoughts and gracious converse."

By REGINALD BLOMFIELD and F. INIGO THOMAS.

THE FORMAL GARDEN IN ENGLAND. With Illustrations. Second Edition. Extra crown 8vo. 7s. 6d. net. Large Paper Edition. Super Royal 8vo. 21s. net.

ACADEMY.—"A daintier little volume than this we have seldom handled."

TIMES.—"A charming book, full of delightful illustrations."

ST. JAMES'S GAZETTE.—"It is a pleasure to read this clever and interesting little book."

SATURDAY REVIEW.—"The reviewer's difficulty with this book consists in the fact that, at whatever page we open, the desire is not so much to express an opinion as to quote, and to go on quoting."

MACMILLAN AND CO., Ltd., LONDON.

www.ingramcontent.com/pod-product-compliance
Lightning Source LLC
Chambersburg PA
CBHW030819020726
47499CB00006B/1982